BURIAL
SUITS

For my Pup, who always told the best scary stories.

<u>Acknowledgements</u>

I have to thank Peggy Mix, who got me reading and writing fiction, The English Department at Indiana University, who made me feel what I did in college was worthwhile, Tony Ardizzone and Cornelia Nixon, who did their best to turn me into a real writer, I hope I'm not embarrassing them too much, and Jesse Marie Roberts at the late Pill Hill Press, that published my first short and didn't scold me for begging my way into one of her anthologies. Special thanks to Garrett Cook, for editing this collection and his advice and encouragement on the stories, and Heather Marie Adkins whose technical assistance saved my sanity.

ISBN-13: 978-1544931159
ISBN-10: 1544931158

Cover Design: Gary Buettner

Table of Contents

Whiteout

"Do you need me to drive?" Derek said, picking at the bandages that covered what used to be his eyes. He couldn't see the blizzard, but he knew the snow was only getting nastier.

Cursing under her breath, Evelyn had turned the wipers all the way up since they'd left the hospital an hour ago. It must really be coming down. Really something to see. "Ouch, so much funnier the first time, dear," Evelyn said.

Derek nodded. She was right, of course, he'd already joked about that when they first left the hospital, when she'd slipped and nearly fallen on her impossible icepick heals getting into the car. In matters of cruelty and merciless humor, he always deferred to his wife's pitiless judgement. "I'll try, in the future, to keep my blind jokes fresh."

"Don't think the world won't appreciate it, Derek. The last thing we need is another sob story. Maybe we can get you a nice dog."

Trying to fake a smile made his eyes hurt, so he tugged, instead, at the collar of his Oxford shirt. Even though his clothes felt too big for him because of the weight he'd lost in the hospital, the combination of car's suffocating heat and his not being able to see the road as they drove, gave him a sour taste in his mouth. Pressing his fist to his lips, he forced down his hospital scrambled eggs and his equally scrambled mind. "The mountains are beautiful this time of year."

Maybe it was just the mild brain damage talking, but Derek could taste her surprise and actually hear her smile. It was the sound of glaciers grinding across stone, digging deep canyons in the rock. Did she perhaps suspect that his blind man's bluff was an elaborate ruse on his part? Despite the searing pain in his eyes, he smiled for real this time, though she would certainly never have given him enough credit to plan and execute such a masterful plan.

Execute? That was an interesting word, wasn't it? Funny that it would come so readily to mind. Execute. He wished that his blindness was a deception in the same way he wished this was just another drive in the country. "We haven't stopped at an intersection in a while and we've made no turns. In this weather, your whole body tenses when we pass drivers going in the other direction, but you haven't done that in maybe an hour. We must be going to the cabin."

"Oh, bravo, Mr. Holmes," she said in her best British accent, which was actually a quite posh delivery that reminded him of the first time he'd ever seen her in college in a play, an English mystery, whose title he couldn't quite remember.

"Elementary, my dear Evelyn."

"I hoped that the cabin would be a nice place for you to recuperate. After all that's happened in the past few weeks, you could probably use a little quiet."

Without the driving to occupy his hands, eyes and mind, Derek's first instinct was to look out the window at the passing scenery, but he faced downward, instead, like he was inspecting his shoes. "Have you decided how you're going to kill me?"

Evelyn gasped, without even breaking character. "I really don't know what you're going on about. I told you that if you kept going into Detroit to take your little church pictures, eventually you would get yourself killed."

"You did tell me that, I'll admit." Derek had been taking black and white pictures of an abandoned church downtown and it had gotten late. Losing the light, he returned to his car only to find himself face to face with a ski-masked man and a .44 Magnum. He never had the chance to tell the man to take his wallet. Without a word, his assailant shoved the gun in his face and pulled the trigger. The police called it a botched carjacking and the doctors said he was lucky to escape with his life. Total and permanent blindness for a professional photographer was, apparently, a real winning lottery ticket.

"They will catch that son of a bitch."

Derek sighed. "About that. There was something else, something that I didn't tell the police."

Evelyn swallowed. "What's that?"

"I saw the man who shot me."

"You...you told them you didn't see the man's face."

"I didn't."

Evelyn sighed with relief. "Well, then..."

"I saw his tattoo. I saw Jimmy's Marine Corps tattoo on his wrist. His sleeve pulled up and I saw it."

"That's...ridiculous. Why would Jimmy, the gardener of all people, want you dead?"

"No reason that I can think of."

"And, besides, those tattoos must be a dime a dozen."

"Not as common as you might think. *Semper Fidelis.* "

"Always faithful," Evelyn said.

"Always faithful. But, Jimmy's tattoo is misspelled. *Smeper Fidelis.* I noticed it before, when he first started working for us, but I couldn't bring myself to mention it. Seemed like such a nice guy and a veteran, so proud of his service. I guess I just didn't want to embarrass him."

Derek heard Evelyn smile her ice queen smile again. "I told that fucking idiot to make sure you were dead."

Derek made a gun of his hand and put it to his temple. "I don't think he was actually a sniper, either." Heart beating faster, he reached for his cellphone in the pocket of his khakis, but it was lost somewhere, probably in his suitcase, uncharged and useless. "Missed me at point blank."

"I don't know how he survived Iraq to be perfectly honest with you and he can barely run the lawnmower, but he fucks like a Viking. You have to get your happy where you can, but I'm not telling you anything you don't already know, am I? How old was that little girl you were screwing?

"Twenty-four in March," he said. "Is that what this is about, then? Sara?"

"Don't say her name." The smile faded from her icy smile, leaving only the ice.

"Normally, I'd try, yet again, to apologize, but you did try to have me assassinated, so..."

"*Assassinated*? Someone certainly has an overinflated sense of himself."

"What do you call it, then?"

"I don't call it anything."

"Okay then, what does Jimmy call it?"

"I can't tell you. You'll just laugh."

"Evelyn, I promise you...I will not laugh."

"Promise?"

"Cross my heart and, well, you know the rest."

"He said that he was going to *ice* you. Seriously, in those exact words. I could barely keep a straight face."

True to his word, Derek did not laugh. "So, I'm curious, what exactly is the new narrative? Did the trigger-happy carjacker from Detroit follow me all the way up here to finish the job?"

"No, thank you very much, that isn't going to work, now. We're off script, so we're going to have to do a little bit of improve comedy. You play the world-famous photographer struck blind at the height of his career. I'll play the loving wife. Ready? And go."

"No one would believe that I tried to kill myself."

"I told the police you had threatened to kill yourself before you left for the city that morning and that I'd seen a gun in your camera bag. I had you on suicide watch at the hospital.

"Insurance doesn't pay in the event of suicide."

"Oh, I know that and you know that, but Jimmy, poor imbecile, does not."

"So what, he kills me, and then you kill him? Something like that?"

"Something exactly like that," she said. "Don't spare my feeling, what do you think of my performance?"

Derek nodded his approval. "I like it," he said, grabbing the steering wheel and cranking it toward him.

The car jerked right, the rear end fishtailing.

Evelyn screamed as the car left the road and, for the first time since the shooting, Derek was glad that he couldn't see.

*****

"Evelyn? Call nine-one-one," Derek said. "I think we crashed, I think. Evie?" His skull felt like it was the wrong shape, like it had been pounded flat by a blacksmith. They were upside-down, blood rushing to his head. Derek undid his safety belt and fell out of his seat. A bolt of pain shot through his left leg, making him scream.

Evelyn.

He found her on the driver's side of the car, sagging in her seatbelt, and pressed his fingers against cheek. "Oh, God," he said. He felt for her pulse, but found nothing but icy skin. Tears burned the corners of his eyes and gave way to a battery acid burn of his wounds. "Evelyn," he said, finally. He undid her seatbelt and gently lowered, making sure she didn't land head first. He cradled her in his arms. "Bitch," he said. He pulled the bandages off his eyes. Sniffing, he wiped his tears with his sleeve. The pain made his stomach churn and shuffle. "Bitch," he said again and gently laid her down. He wished he could see her one last time.

Derek reached for his cellphone, but it was gone. "Shit." He patted his blazer pocket, knowing that he would not find it. He dug in Evelyn's purse for her phone, but could not find it either. If someone tried to call, the phone would ring. He imagined Jimmy calling. Jimmy, his would-be assassin. Would he come to the rescue? Not likely.

He ran his hands through his hair. He felt something wet on his head. The pain made him dizzy. In the dark, it was unbearable and he wanted to puke.

Derek struggled and pushed the passenger door open. He crawled out into the snow. It was deep, almost to his elbows when he was on all-fours. How deep was that? A foot? Two?

Bracing himself on the car door, Derek lifted himself to a standing position. The pain was too much, though and he collapsed.

"Not going to work," he said. He got back on his hands and knees and crawled to the back of the car. The snow there was deeper than it had been by the passenger door and it was brushing his chin as he crawled. He could feel the cold soaking through his pants and into his numb skin.

At the back of the car, he felt for the car's track in the snow. Finding it quickly, he began to crawl along feeling his way. The trough in the snow went for several feet and he imagined himself crawling onto pavement any minute and either walking down the mountain or flagging a car.

A bit of panic jolted his stomach as he imagined Jimmy stopping for him. There was no way around it. That would just have to be something they dealt with later. He shook his head and a clump of snow fell down his neck. Cursing the cold, he continued to crawl.

The track ended.

No road, no rescue, not even Jimmy waiting to kill him and make it look like a suicide.

Derek screamed, but it was lost in the howling wind. Derek was shivering and his teeth chattered like he'd only see in cartoons. He imagined himself turning blue with icicles hanging off his nose and ears.

Derek.

The voice was so subtle and quiet that he thought he was imagining things. "Ev...Evelyn?"

The wind moaned and Derek shivered with fear as much as cold. He imagined Evelyn's body sitting in a heap back in the car. Worse, he imagined it not in the car, but staggering through the snow towards him. Eyes as pale as the snow that he crawled through.

How hard had he cracked his head?

"You're dead, honey. I'm sorry, but you're dead."

He tilted his head and listened. Someone had told him once that blind people's other senses usually sharpened to account for the lost sight. Maybe it took a while. The insulating blanket of snow seemed to mute everything except the moan of the wind and his own heartbeat.

Got to go back to the car, he thought, not liking the idea one bit. If he had to kick Evelyn out into the snow and lock the Lexus's doors then he would. Maybe he could just honk the horn until help came. He almost laughed at the thought.

He carefully turned in a circle like a dog and followed his own tracks back. They had collapsed some and filled in some, so a few times he found himself off his track. He crawled over something. Something sharp that poked his numb knee through his pants.

Cellphone?

He quickly dug in the snow and pulled the offending item free.

Evelyn's high heel.

Derek dropped it like a tarantula and wiped his hands on his snow-slick blazer. How the fuck did that get out here? He clamped one hand over his mouth to keep from screaming and listened.

The wind and his heartbeat. Only the wind and his heartbeat.

He swallowed hard, trying to stand up. He always imagined if faced with a life or death situation that he would be able to hop right up and run on a broken leg, a sprained ankle or other equally debilitating injury.

He collapsed in the snow like a poorly made snowman. He felt sleepy, not just tired from the wreck and the crawling, but sleepy, drugged, anesthetized. He wondered if Evelyn could have slipped something in his last Starbucks. No, he thought, it was the cold. He was going to freeze to death out here.

He held the shoe tight in his grasp. He squeezed it. A logical explanation. Not even logical, at this point, on the verge of freezing he would take anything at this point. Any explanation. Illogical or not.

He must've dragged it with him when he crawled from the car or maybe it had been thrown from the car when it rolled.

"There you go," he said, lips frozen. "There are two per...perfectly good explanations." He nodded, picturing himself as Jack Nicolson at the end of *The Shining,* insane and frozen to death.

He crawled back to the car, almost missing it as the snow rose and continued to drift, filling in his tracks.

Evelyn was still in the car which both relieved and unsettled him. He struggled to pull the door shut. When he got as comfortable as he could, he stopped to think. He'd assumed that the car had come in a straight line from the road, so that any tracks he followed would lead back to the road. If the car had spun, it could be any direction back to the road. "Fuck," he said, wishing he hadn't thought of it.

He shivered. He tried to turn the car on, but the key turned in the ignition but did nothing else. Not even as much as a click to tell him that there was anything under the hood. No heat, then.

His hand had gone beyond numb to burning. He hadn't brought gloves, but Evelyn had. He felt around until he found her and then continued until he found her pockets. The gloves were inside.

He imagined the feeling of cold hands on his. He thought that if something were to touch him now, he would scream and be unable to stop.

He couldn't move.

Derek tried to calm his breathing down. Outside the wind seemed to be working in the opposite direction. The car rocked with the wind.

A cold hand touched his.

Derek screamed, falling back to the passenger side, the gloves gripped tight against his chest. "Evelyn? Evelyn?"

Nothing.

Derek imagined her watching him with eyes like two flecks of crystal.

She moved because the car rocked with the wind, he told himself, but he pulled his legs up and rocked himself into a warm, little ball. His head felt like it was spinning. Was this even real? Was this happening? It felt like a nightmare. It felt like a bad dream.

Derek.

Derek. You're going the wrong way.

Derek snapped to consciousness. He'd fallen asleep. He looked around by sheer reflex, but could see nothing. It took him a minute to remember where he was. His stomach dropped. "You're going the wrong way," he said, feeling the words on his numb lips. He stretched out from the ball that he had wrapped himself in, though he couldn't feel anything from the waist down.

I'm going to freeze to death, he thought

"Going the wrong way," he said. "Wrong way. Okay. What's the right way?" He was convinced that Evelyn was trying to help him. He reached in the backseat, found her coat and pulled it on. It was tight, but he managed to button it up. He would go the other way, the way the car pointed.

Evelyn's coat was so warm, he wondered why he hadn't thought of that before. He shook his head. He was his own worst enemy.

No, he thought, my wife and her boyfriend are my worst enemies.

He pushed the passenger door open. It was harder this time as the snow had piled even higher. Derek crawled out. He shut the door, turned toward the front of the car and began to make his way through the snow.

The wind was louder than it was before, but he could hear the creak and snap of branches above his head. Bits of ice and snow fell out of the trees in clumps.

Derek.

He didn't stop this time. He hurried as fast as he could on his hands and knees.

Hurry Derek.

"I'm going as fast as I can," he said, gasping for breath. His lungs burned.

Jimmy is coming.

Derek got to his feet and ran. The numbness in his lower body helped as he staggered into the storm.

He got three steps before he fell through the ice.

The water was needles in his skin. He tumbled forward and went under, smashing face-first through a thin layer of ice. His hands sunk into frozen mud on the bottom of the creek that he had fallen in. He jerked his head up searching for air, but only managed to strike his head on the bottom of the ice.

Bitch, he thought. Bitch.

Derek got his good leg under him and stood up. His shoulder caught the ice on way and he felt it break the skin and the hot blood running down his arm. His eyes were on fire. He stumbled backward out of the water and fell on his back in the snow. He gasped for air.

"Evelyn," he said. "Bitch."

She's still trying to kill me, he thought. I'm going to die out here.

He turned his head and found that the snow was so deep that his body was completely beneath the level of the snow. The wind was not so bad down here, though it screamed in the trees above his head. Shivering, freezing, he lay in the snow.

Somewhere, nearby, he heard Queen's *Bohemian Rhapsody* play.

Evelyn's phone.

Derek scrambled onto his hands and knees and crawled toward where the phone was ringing. It was amazing that he could hear it with all the snow. He had to be a good thirty feet from the car, how the hell did the phone get that far away?

It was thrown in the crash, he thought, trying not to think about it.

He fell on the spot where the phone had been, but the ringing stopped. "No, no, no," he said digging into the snow with hands that felt like slabs of uncooked meat. He couldn't find it.

The phone rang again.

It wasn't in front of him, he sloughed through the snow and dug down. He could barely hold the phone. He punched the answer button. "Help me, we crashed," Derek said.

"Derek?" It was Jimmy. "Where's Evelyn?"

Derek hung the phone up and quickly dialed nine-one-one.

"911 emergency," the woman's voice said.

"Thank God," Derek said, trying to keep it together. "We were in a crash, my wife is dead, I'm freezing..."

"Please relax, nobody needs another sob story, sir..."

That was strange. Derek stared at the phone. "Evelyn?" He pressed the phone against his ear. "Hello?"

The phone was dead. He dropped it in the snow.

It rang again. He grabbed it up off the ground and answered it. It was Jimmy. Derek thought quickly. "Thank God you called back. We got cut off."

"Where's Evelyn?"

"We had a wreck. She's...," Derek said, stopping himself suddenly. "Uh, she's hurt really bad we need help."

"Let me talk to her."

"She...she's unconscious."

"Oh, Christ. Where are you?"

"About a half-hour from the cabin," he said. "Off the road."

"I'll be there in twenty minutes," Jimmy said clicking the phone off.

Derek's heart leapt. He stuffed the phone in his pocket and crawled back to the car. Evelyn was still trying to kill him, he thought. She'd led him into the water. She had hidden the phones and made it not work. Now, Jimmy was on his way. God only knew what he would do when he found Evelyn dead.

"Honey, I really feel like this relationship isn't working. It isn't you, or your boyfriend, it's me. I feel like we've grown apart. You aren't going to kill me, sweetie. Not going to fucking happen."

When he got back to the car, he stopped to make sure her body was still there. It was. He grabbed her by the arm and dragged her out into the snow.

*****

Jimmy found the place where the car had gone off the road in fifteen minutes. The snow had covered the tracks, but it had stuck to them as well and they stood out like fingerprints. Jimmy screeched to a halt. He dug the Beretta out of the glove box and got out of the truck.

From the side of the road, Jimmy could see the car in the snow. He couldn't believe that it travelled so far in one piece. It was facing away from the road and it was upside down.

He didn't see that prick Derek, but a body lay in the snow nearby. A woman.

"Evelyn!" Jimmy slid down the hill nearly wiping out and ran to the where Evelyn lay sprawled. The snow was pink with blood.

He squatted down in the thigh-deep snow and searched for a pulse with stiffening fingers, but he found nothing. She was dead.

"Fucking Derek," he said, pulling the gun from his coat. He pulled back the slide, putting a round in the chamber. "I'm going to fucking kill you," he said, his voice carrying above the wind.

He couldn't have gotten too far, that little shit. Blind man stumbling around in the fucking woods.

Jimmy scanned the woods, but didn't see anything.

Evelyn coughed. Her head moved.

"Baby," Jimmy said dropping to his knees. He was face to face with her. "Oh baby, I thought you were dead."

"I am," Derek said and stabbed him in the face with Evelyn's high heel.

Stumbling back in the snow, Jimmy clutched at his eye, screaming.

Derek could feel Jimmy's hot blood spattered across his hand. It felt so good and warm.

Jimmy screamed.

Why isn't he shooting me? At his feet, he found the answer. "Dropped your gun." Derek picked it up. It felt good in his hand, not as good as the blood, but you took your happy where you could get it.

"I came to help, you, man," Jimmy said. "My eye, I can't see."

"Nobody wants another sob story," Derek said and shot Jimmy in the face. Jimmy hit the ground softly. Derek aimed in the direction of the moaning and squeezed off three more shots.

Derek walked toward the sound of Jimmy's truck idling. He imagined himself driving down the steep, windy mountain roads, weaving back and forth and laughed. He cradled the gun in both hands feeling its warmth against his body. He thought he heard a voice or two in the wind behind him, but he didn't not stop and didn't look back. Nothing to see anyway.

A Zombie is Worth a Thousand Words

After the armed guards passed, Sara crept out to the railing of the zombie retaining wall, hooked her climbing rope to it and dropped the line over the edge. The autumn night felt crisp and cool, but the concrete and the steel railing were freezing. Sara thought she should have worn gloves. Too late now. Her adrenaline was surging and she felt like a ninja.

"I really have to advise against suicide as a career move, Sara. You took the most amazing photograph of the twentieth century," Dr. Hillman had said. *The Mother of all Zombies*, he meant. The first photographic proof of the undead. Her meal ticket. Before the worldwide zombie infestation, it was the first real proof of life after death. Afterward, it became a kind of rallying cry for the Zombie Defensive.

Sara hooked her harness to the drop line, checked her camera, her gun, and her ammunition. Maybe she was overdoing it with the climbing harness. The wall stood only twenty feet tall, just about two stories. It was like climbing out her apartment window to the street below. Though, come to think of it, she'd never done that either. Sara tested her harness. The guards took fifteen minutes to make the circuit between perimeter stations. If she was going, then it was now.

Her photograph, the mother springing from her funeral coffin, attacking her son, was as famous as the

Raising the Flag at Iwo Jima, the student in front of the tank at Tianaman Square or the sailor kissing the nurse on VJ day. The moment she had captured would either have been the end of humanity or the start of humanity's greatest struggle. It made her a celebrity in photojournalist circles.

But moments, all moments, pass.

"Nothing that I've done since has even come close," she'd told him. "I need something...something really fucking big."

"What you're suggesting is against the law."

"I can't pay my rent." Sara tried to read his face. She had spent her entire life as a photographer, trying to read and understand people's expressions, to understand and therefore capture, elusive moments. She watched Dr. Hillman's face and could not read him. "Call the cops, then," she said. Sara left the psychiatrist's office and did not return.

Sara stared down into the darkness at the bottom of the massive wall. She could see the blue tops of the pine trees, but she could not see the ground. Would the guards shoot her if they found her here? The sign said that lethal force was authorized beyond this point, but would they actually shoot her?

Sara took a deep breath and let herself go.

She bounced down the side of the steel-reinforced concrete structure in graceful, zero-gravity hops, trying her best not to make a sound. She obviously did not want the guards to hear her and she especially did not want anything that might be hiding in the woods below to hear her.

Sara had spent time as a photojournalist in Rwanda and she felt that knew how to survive in hostile conditions. She'd spent more than time in Rwanda. Sara had spent nearly all the money she had made off the photo, trying to shoot something non-zombie-related. Trying to be a real journalist.

It had been several years since Sara had done any rock climbing, but as she lowered herself to the ground, she thought that it seemed to be coming back to her.

Something snagged her foot, the heel of her hiking boot caught in a crevice in the concrete wall.

She flipped over, her head cracking against the wall, her feet suddenly above her. Stars danced before her eyes like in a Tom and Jerry cartoon. Arms dangling, Sara felt her shoulder bags slipping over her arms.

"Fuck!" The reflex of a lifetime of experience carrying a camera kicked in and she snatched at her camera bag, catching it just as her gun fell away into darkness. She would have to find it when she got down to the ground.

A blinding light exploded in the night.

Sara covered her eyes with one hand. What was she going to do now?

She realized that they light wasn't trained directly on her. They didn't know she was here. Had they found the rope?

Sara unhooked her harness and fell. She had the distinct impression that she wasn't falling, that she was hanging in the air and that the ground raced up to meet her.

Stunned, she lay on the ground for a few minutes, trying to find her camera. Had she landed on it? No. She felt the familiar padded shape of her camera bag. Okay. She spit out a mouthful of dirt and pine needles. Everything was going to be fine.

The light moved, darting across the concrete wall like a drunken UFO.

Gotta move, she thought. Get your fat ass up. Sara rolled over onto her hands, pushed herself up to her feet.

Another light joined the first, crisscrossing beams like a Hollywood movie premiere. One of them stopped on the dangling rope.

Forget that, then.

Sara sprung to her feet and scrambled toward the trees in a shaky, zigzag line. She wondered if she had a concussion. If she did, then she did. There was nothing to be done about it now. She had to get as far from the wall as she could. The gun was gone and now so was the rope. Her defense and her way out. Didn't matter, she still had her camera. Grinning, Sara ran like an escaped convict.

***

Sara tried to stay alert, to keep her head in the game, but the endless walking, without as much as one zombie to call her own, began to take its toll. She'd slept in a tree the night before, not even sure that she could get to sleep, but even sitting up in the cradling branches of an oak tree, a creepy *Halloween*-type tree, she was out in minutes. Now, she walked. Her mind wandering as uncertainly as she did.

Her career was flatlining and she needed something intense to jolt it back to life. Zombies weren't as common in the outside world as they had once been, now to find the walking dead you had to come to the reservations. People were forgetting about them. Rumors spread that the government would clear the reservations soon and then the zombies would be gone forever. She needed something shocking to revive her career. The problem with the career defibrillator, if you wanted to dissect that particular metaphor, was that it stopped the heart to reset it. She didn't know if it was possible for her career. Would it have to die to be reborn?

"I'm a fraud," she said aloud, and the sound of her own voice startled her. She ran her hands through her short, black hair, and locked her fingers together on the top of her head. She sighed hard. What the fuck was she doing here? What the fuck?

Sara had taken the picture, of course. But.

But.

But, it had practically been an accident. She had carried a camera everywhere she went since she was nine-years-old. In this instance though, at age thirty-six, her camera phone happened to be out, calling her boyfriend, Charlie, to see why he was late for his own Aunt Theresa's funeral, when the old lady popped up and went after her own son.

Sara didn't even remember actually snapping the pic. For all she knew, she might have just flinched in panic.

Sara froze. Had she heard something? She stood perfectly still, held her breath and listened.

Long seconds passed, leaving her caught between dread and anticipation. It had been so long since she'd actually seen a zombie for real, that the thought of it repulsed her, even as she hoped she would find something.

Something *unusual*.

When she was reasonably sure that she was alone, she continued around the edge of the bare woods, quietly scanning the empty fields she passed.

By the time she reached the first town, a few small homes, a trailer park, and a few businesses, spread out from the main road like the grease stain from a fallen potato chip, her legs ached and she had a rock in her boot.

She moved from the relative safety of the treeline to the middle of the highway. From there, she could at least see if anything was sneaking up on her, but she saw nothing.

A child's hand print, maroon with dried blood, stained the storm door of the mobile home closest to the main road. Sara snapped several pictures of it. In the yard, a blue plastic kiddie pool sat, still full of green-black water. Something floated in the muck.

Sara brought her camera to her eye.

It moved.

Green water sloshed over the side of the pool and ran down to the dried grass on which it sat.

Sara lowered her camera and took a step closer. Had it actually moved? It could have just been the wind.

The water moved again. Not the wind.

Sara took several quick steps backwards, raising her camera, hands shaking. This could be it, she thought. Whatever came up out of that water, she would shoot it.

Then what?

She didn't know. She would shoot it and run.

Run where?

Fuck *where*. Photo first, then *where*.

She hoped it was a dead child. Even as her gorge rose, even as her hands shook and her mouth grew dry, she hoped it was a dead child, a little girl in a flowered dress with one tooth missing from a wide smile. Her flesh would be pale like the underside of a fish, ribs showing through just above her bloated toddler belly.

The water moved again and Sara ran.

Sara did not stop until she was well out of town. She found an enormous stone, probably dug out of the ground by a farmer plowing his field, and sat on it to rest. She undid her shoe, shook it upside down, which reminded her of her harrowing descent down the security wall and then put her show back on. She tried to drink a warm bottle of water from her bag, but her hands shook so intensely that she only managed to dump half of it down the front of her jacket.

Okay, that didn't go to well.

The little girl was coming.

Sara jumped, dropping her water bottle.

The road behind her was empty. Her hand was pressed so tightly to her face that it ached.

"No little girl," Sara said. This time, her voice was reassuring in the quiet. "No wet foot prints. No nothing."

Sara slung her pack on her back and headed back down the road the way she had been going, out of town.

She turned to face the town again. The little girl? No. Should she go back? She glanced to the road that led away from the town, something caught her eye.

A square blue sign with an H. A hospital.

Sara turned away from the town and followed the sign.

*****

Lying on her belly in an overgrown shrubbery on a hill, Sara watched the zombies mill around the hospital parking lot below. The building was shiny and white with aluminum trim giving it the appearance of a giant White Castle restaurant. There were more zombies in one place than she had ever seen before. She shot a dead cop lumbering around on a leg and a half. She saw several nurses and she regretted that they no longer wore the white uniforms and the little hats. It would have seemed more classic that way, she thought. Hell, maybe they never wore those hats. She would google that when she got back, just out of curiosity. She saw a young woman, dead of course, wearing a *PRO-LIFE* t-shirt. "Oh, you ironic bitch, you."

Then she saw him.

The man limped in a wobbly circle in the parking lot pulling his IV along behind him. Despite rolling on four little wheels, it had not fallen over. His head hung down, mouth open. He wore an industrial green hospital robe and pajama pants. His gray hair was only a shade darker than his gray skin and his torso hung open having long since torn open the stitches, that held whatever procedure he'd had done, closed.

He was the most beautiful thing she had ever seen.

Sara zoomed in close and shot off several pictures and then crawled back into the cover of the shrub. Checking the pictures on the view screen, she almost started giggling. They were beyond perfect. She had hoped to maybe get a Time magazine cover, maybe something that would reignite interest in her earlier picture, but this, this could be a whole fucking book. Shaking with anticipation, she checked the pictures of her favorite patient.

They were...okay. Nothing wrong with them, just...okay.

The other zombies she had shot were perfect, but they were much closer to her than he was. She was shooting down at them, but it did stand out too much in the photos, but the patient was farther away and it seemed to emphasize the height difference.

She had to get this picture. This was the picture she came for.

Sara belly crawled back to her vantage point at the edge of the shrubs. She watched as the zombies made their pointless orbits around the parking lot. Her patient came very close to the Emergency Room doors as he came around each time. If she could get inside the building, she could shoot him as he came near her. To do this, though, she would have to go inside the hospital. Zombie central.

She smiled. This was going to make her career, she thought. These pictures. Get these pictures and get the fuck out of the reservation. The magazine editors would shit there pants. When they cleaned out the reservations, this would be the last photographic record of any of this. She found that she was smiling so much that it hurt her face.

She crawled backwards out of the shrub and ran, hunched over into the woods that surrounded the hospital. From the back of the building, she found an loading dock, climbed in and found her way into the building. Things had happened fast here, there has been no time to secure the place, no barricades like you saw in some of the major cities.

Emergency Room---Follow the Red Line

Sara could see the sign from the meager sunlight that filtered in through the open loading dock. She could make out the line on the floor even in the darker insides of the hospital. She hurried, but tried to stay quiet. She could not even imagine what might be inside that drove the other zombies outside.

She passed through the cafeteria, a large open space full of dining tables that smelled like rotten food into a large waiting area that smelled like rotten corpses.

The front wall of the Emergency Room was made of large windows and the sunlight poured in. Sara was glad to be out of the dark recesses of the hospital and back to where she could see. She stood silently behind a column, letting her eyes readjust to the light.

Hand Washing is the Best Way to Prevent the Spread of Germs!

"Amen to that," she said, adjusting her camera.

She peeked around the column to see where in his circuit her patient was. She did not see him which meant that he was just coming around.

She slid out from behind the column, hunched down to catch him from a low angle and waited.

The patient passed the window.

He was still wearing his hospital admit bracelet. Fucking cool.

Sara snapped pictures as he passed. These pics were perfect, she could tell.

She put her hand down to help herself up and she felt something wet.

"What the...:

Several small, wet footprints led right up behind her.

The little girl.

Stop that shit, she thought. There was no little girl.

Sara slung her camera over her neck and ran.

Something caught her before she made two steps. She went down hard on the tile floor. Her head swam with pain. Her leg burned with agony.

Something was...biting her. She rolled to look.

The little girl wasn't missing any teeth in her big smile.

*****

Sergeant Jiminez was standing the wall with that kid, Calhoun, when the female zombie shambled out of the pines toward them. They'd been posted there where they found the climbing rope, assuming whoever had gone over, would try to climb back. The search and rescue teams had turned up nothing. She looked fresh and Sergeant Jiminez figured it was probably time to call the search teams back.

"Look at that bitch, Sarge, she has a camera. I think she's a tourist. Bitch wants to take our picture," Calhoun said.

"Stow that shit, Private, she was a human being once, try to show a little respect." The Sergeant wondered what was on that camera. He thought when they moved out into the reservation tomorrow as part of the first wave of clean up, then maybe he would find the camera and see what was on it. As many zombies as he'd seen in the service, it always creeped him out that each one almost told a story. They seemed to carry their own epitaph. He shouldered his rifle and put one round into her forehead.

Vultures

While Ray bled, the man circled.

"I don't know if this makes any difference to you," the man said, his long, bony hands behind his back, "but you have my solemn promise that I will not eat you until you are well and truly dead."

"Fuck you," Ray said, trying to spit the words, but coming up with only a mouthful of desert dust.

"Such language," the man said, smacking his thin lips. "You're nearing the end. Shouldn't you be making peace with your God?"

"Not really religious," Ray said. "Besides, what're you, the Devil now?"

If the man was auditioning for the role of the Antichrist, then he definitely had the look right. Impossibly tall and thin, he moved with his arms tucked behind him in a way that it made his hunched shoulders look like folded wings. Bald was a word wasted on him, he had no hair that Ray could see. No eyebrows. Eyelashes. Nothing. Sharp and curved like a meat hook, his enormous nose dominated his pale, wrinkled face. "I never said that."

Ray looked back at his car, crashed just off the Nevada highway. The trail of blood had mostly sunk into the sand. "You're going to eat me after I'm dead. You're some kind of ghoul, right?"

"*Ghul* means *demon* in Arabic, did you know that? Are you sure you're not religious?"

"Are you sure you're not a necrophiliac?"

The man was in Ray's face so fast, that he hardly had time to blink. His breath smelled of rotten meat. The man's eyes were yellow and had no pupils. "Would you like me to eat you, now, while you can still feel it?"

Ray trembled beneath the weight of the man's gaze. "No."

"What?"

Ray cleared his throat and spoke louder. "No."

"See how easy it is to be polite?" The man continued circling. "You probably only have a few minutes left before you pass out and die of blood loss."

"Are you a doctor, now?"

"A surgeon, maybe, a coroner perhaps, but most assuredly a gastronome."

Ray shifted against the rock. "I don't know what that is."

The man smiled like a naughty child with a secret. "A gastronome is a gourmet, a connoisseur of fine foods."

Ray dropped his head back against the rock. He thought maybe the man was right. Not long now. He felt his body shaking. "Tell me one thing, please."

"Of course."

Ray grinned. "You aren't going to fuck me when I'm dead, are you?"

The man pounced on Ray. "I told you..."

Ray brought the rock he'd been holding up and bashed the man's skull. He hit it again and again. The thing died without another word.

Ray sighed. The desert really was as peaceful a place to die as any.

They Never Stop Swimming

By the time the detectives, Chambers and Paulson, got to the dorm, a crowd of UMASS students, tanned and drunk, had already amassed around the yellow police tape, not sure there was anything to see, but determined not to miss it. Spring Break was all but over, classes started bright and early in the morning, but a few revelers seemed unwilling to let it go.

Detective Ernie Chambers, on the job twenty-eight years, hated an audience. He knew that the kids, hell most people, raised on a steady diet of CSI, expected cops to be young and good-looking, two things that Ernie knew that he was not. Ernie had reached the fifty-fifth year in the marathon of life and he had accumulated nothing to show for it but a gray mustache and a sixty pound belly. "These kids missing *Law and Order* for this?"

"Must smell blood in the water," Detective Mike Paulson said. Anybody seeing the two detectives together would immediately suspect them of being father and son. Mike was in his thirties, but passed for twenty when he shaved. People often underestimated him because he was skinny and young looking.

Looking like Laurel and Hardy, the two detectives parked the car in a fire lane, and headed up the cement walk to the front of the dorm where several uniforms were standing. "Hey, Jeffries, what's the what?"

Officer Jeffries looked paler than usual. "Let me show you," he said, leading them through the lobby to the elevator. He punched the up button and waited. "You guys eat?"

"No," Mike said.

"You offering to buy us dinner?" Ernie chuckled.

"No, I just thought I should warn you."

"Duly warned," Mike said, smiling to Ernie. The uniforms always made out like *this* was the worst they'd ever seen.

"Okay, so the RA For floor seven..."

"Whoa, Professor Marvel, talk slow I didn't go to college," Ernie said.

"RA. *Is resident advisor,*" Officer Jeffries said.

"Den mother. College boy babysitter," Mike said, when Ernie still seemed perplexed.

"Okay, go ahead," Ernie said, pulling out his little notebook and his pen.

"RA Says he saw the victim, one Andrew Elten, come in last night at 12:30. Tonight at 7:04, RA Is headed to the john..."

"7:04 on the dot? This guy's pea shooter have a clock on it?"

"Clock on the wall in the hall supposed to help students get to class on time."

"Does it work?"

"Not for one Andrew Elten, because at 7:04 on the dot, RA passes victim's room sees water leaking out from the under the door."

The elevator opened. The three men got in and punched the seventh floor button. *The Girl from Impanema* droned in the background as the elevator climbed.

"Broken fishtank? Signs of a struggle?" Ernie scratched his head with his pen.

"Broken waterpipe?" Mike shrugged.

"No and no."

The elevator opened on the seventh floor. Officer Jeffries led the two detectives down the hall to where a large water stain soaked the green carpet. It sloshed as they stepped through it. "RA drains the lizard comes back to call maintenance and sees blood."

"Ouch," Ernie said.

"Ouch is right. A ton of blood. He calls 911. 911 calls us, we arrive, open the door with the passkey that is so graciously provided to us, and..." Officer Jeffries pushed the door open. "....we find this."

"The fuck?" Mike leaned into the room without actually stepping through the door.

"I just work here." Jeffries backed up, holding his hands up.

The body, or what was left of it, lay in a pool of bloody water in the middle of the floor. Opening the door caused a wave that swept across the whole room. A crescent shape roughly the size of half a large pizza was missing from the man's midsection. An organ that Ernie could not identify hung from the wound. Ribs, like little white fingers, protruded from the red mess of the deceased's insides.

"The body has obviously been dumped here from, I don't know, somewhere else," Ernie said, sniffing. "Smell that? That's sea water." He pointed to the floor by the bed. "Look, I think that's seaweed."

Jeffries said. "The RA said he never left."

Mike shook his head. "RA is full of shit, then, where is he?"

"Paramedics have him. He's sucking oxygen. He freaked when we opened the door."

"Smart man," Ernie said, and then to Mike. "You know what that looks like, right?"

"Yeah, I know what it looks like, but we are a few miles from the ocean. Very few sharks in Boston city limits," Mike said, smiling.

"Aquarium?"

"I think someone would have noticed."

Ernie stepped back out into the hallway, wiped sweat from his forehead.

Mike moved to step into the room, thought better of it and instead joined Ernie in the hallway. "What do you think?"

Ernie shrugged. "Guy comes home from spring break..."

"Suitcases are on the floor next to the bed," Mike added.

"Guy comes home from spring break somebody gets in his room. They struggled, break the fish tank..."

"What fish tank?"

"There's a hundred gallons of seawater on the floor, fucking seaweed. I bet if we look under the bed we'll find a couple of expensive salt water fish..."

"Where's the tank?"

"Broken"

"Where the glass?"

"Cleaned up." Ernie scratched his head with his pen. "He cuts up our guy and...wait, where's the missing, uh, flesh?"

Mike looked around the hallway. "Jeffries, where's the meat?"

Jeffries shrugged.

"Okay," Ernie said, raising his voice so the other cops could hear him. "Shopping list: milk, bread and the missing chunk of meat."

The uniforms headed to search.

Mike leaned against the wall. "I don't buy it. That room is a fucking mess. Who cleans up broken glass, but leaves all that water and blood.

They talked about it for a few more minutes until Jeffries reappeared carrying something.

"You find it?"

"No, I got you guys some waders." He handed them two pairs of thigh high rubber boots.

"We going fishing?" Ernie struggled to pull his pair on.

"Seems like it," Mike said.

They went into the room.

"You know what I'm not seeing?" Mike made a sweeping gesture.

"A place to put a hundred gallon fish tank?"

"Yeah, sorry, Ernie."

"No worries. Where'd the water come from?"

"Fucked if I know. Hey, maybe we're looking at this the wrong way."

"So?"

"So, maybe somebody put this water here on purpose."

"Why?"

"Maybe for the same reason they cut a chunk of this guy out to look like a shark bite. They went through a ton of trouble to make this look like a fucking shark attack."

"Why?"

"I don't know, but I sure would like to know where this guy went for spring break."

Ernie picked a camera bag up from the pile of luggage near the bed. "Maybe he took some pictures."

Ernie and Mike waited until the coroner came and took the body and the Crime Scene guys started on the place, before they took the camera and left.

They got a booth at a nearby diner and sat down with the camera. Mike flipped through the pictures. "Nothing. Nothing. Nothing. Jesus, some people just take pictures of anything. Doesn't anyone just remember stuff anymore?"

Ernie grunted as the waitress brought his coffee and Mike's chili.

"You're eating?"

"Yeah, so?"

"After that? Chili at midnight?"

"Chili at anytime. Chili for breakfast. Chili for lunch. I would brush my teeth with chili."

"Aw, c'mon," Ernie said, "you're just exaggerating for comedic effect."

Ernie took the camera and flipped through some more pictures. "Looks like he went to Mexico to do some fishing. Ever go to Mexico?"

"No, you?"

"Yeah, you ever hear of a Tijuana Zebra?"

"That isn't something obscene is it?"

"Naw, just a donkey painted with stripes. 'Course, I can't vouch for what the donkey was doing before he got painted."

Mike shook his head and ate his chili.

"Looks like he went with two other guys." Ernie held the camera up so that Mike could see. "We ought to talk to those hombres."

"Si, senor."

Ernie continued flipping through the pictures. "Oh, shit."

"What?"

"I don't know if you are old enough to see this, Mikey." Ernie held the camera out to him.

"Looks like they met some girls in Mexico."

"Think any of those girls have a jealous boyfriend? Mike? Mike!"

"Sorry, man. Damn, I should go to Mexico."

"Jealous boyfriend?"

"Maybe. Angry pimp?"

"Think those are working girls?"

"I don't know. They are definitely working in these pictures. And that, that right there, that costs extra."

"We should find those other two guys." Mike said, pouring hot sauce in his bowl.

"I bet you a bowl of chili that those two guys are the last two people he called."

Mike called Jeffries, got the number from the victims thankfully waterproof cellphone. "Pete and Adam."

"Pete and Re-Pete," Ernie said. His own phone rang "Yeah. Really? No shit? Thanks for getting to me so quick."

"What's that about?"

"Coroner. You are going to shit when I tell you this. Cause of death was that gaping chest wound."

"Really? I kinda thought that..."

"Real shark bite," Ernie said.

"Bullshit."

"No bullshit. Coroner, Faraday? Ex-Navy. Said he saw these all the time. Probably a tiger shark."

The both sat in silence.

Mike looked down at the camera. "Uh, is *this* a tiger shark?"

The picture showed the three men holding a large, dead shark up on the end of a cable.

"Call Pete."

Mike told Pete to lock his door and stay put, then he called for a patrol car to meet them at the scene.

"I know who did this," Ernie said, heading out to the car.

"Wow, I'm all ears."

"The guy who took the picture."

"How you figure?"

"Maybe he's an enviro-Nazi, sees these guys kill the shark, goes overboard, no pun intended and comes to the states to kill these three, make it look like Mother Nature's revenge."

Mike shrugged.

They got there ahead of the patrol car, but didn't wait.

"So, is Pete a suspect?" Mike shut his car door.

Ernie shrugged. "I guess he must be. Either he's the doer or Adam or both of them or someone else entirely."

Mike chuckled, shaking his head. "That certainly narrows it down."

Somewhere on one of the upper floors of the building someone screamed.

They both drew their pieces and headed to the front door of the building. Once inside, they saw that two different flights of stairs led upstairs, one inside and then another outside that led up the back.

"I'll take the front," Mike said, darting up the stairs.

Ernie remembered when he could run like that. He hurried to the back stairs.

The backdoor of the building was flanked by two dumpsters, the air thick with the smell of hot garbage. Ernie turned to go up the stairs and realized that he could see the windows of the top floor apartments from the back parking lot. He paused at the bottom of the back stairs, took a deep breath and readied himself for the stairs or for the heart attack whichever came first.

Something moved behind the curtains on the top floor. At first, he thought it was Mike or this Pete character, but as he watched he saw that it was neither.

A dark shaped glided by the window.

"Holy shit."

*****

Mike and Ernie sat on the curb as the crime scene guys headed up to Pete's apartment. "Same shit?" Ernie sat, his forearms on his knees, hands dangling.

"Worse."

"Did he have a fishtank?"

Mike shook his head. "You and your fucking fishtank."

Ernie shrugged, forced a smile. "Fuck you."

"Fuck you to infinity." Mike seemed pale. He took a drag on his cigarette, stared at it.

"I thought you quit."

"After that shit," he said, gesturing toward the top floor," I just re-started and I'm thinking about doubling up. I hope I get cancer. I hope I get cancer and die, just so I know I won't wind up like that poor prick up there."

Ernie nodded. "I guess Pete isn't our guy, huh?"

"Yeah, I guess we can say Pete has what you might call the ultimate alibi."

Ernie took a deep breath and exhaled. "Adam?"

"Not unless he can juggle chainsaws."

"I saw something," Ernie said, covering his mouth with his hand so only Mike could hear him. The last thing he wanted was to explain this to one of the uniforms that were milling around the scene, stretching yellow police tape between two massive oaks.

Mike turned his head. Ernie could see in his eyes that he didn't think that anything he had to tell him would make a difference. "What?"

"You're not going to believe me."

Mike smiled for real. "At this point I will believe anything you have to tell me."

"I saw a shark."

Ernie paused not sure what he was waiting for.

"And...?"

"In the window. It just...moved past the window like...I don't know...like I was looking into an aquarium. It just...swam by."

"Now," Mike said after sitting quietly for a long time. "How exactly does that work, do you think?"

"I don't think there's a form for this."

"College guys kill shark. Dead shark kills college guys?"

"Dead shark."

"Are we talking ghosts?"

"Ghost shark?"

"I found this," Mike said, holding out a small evidence bag. Ernie took it, looked inside. It contained a shark tooth with a leather strap wrapped around it like a necklace."

"It's the teeth, isn't it?"

Mike took the other tooth out of his jacket. "Two teeth, two guys."

"Why didn't it take the teeth?"

"Maybe it can't."

"How do we stop this, Ernie?"

Ernie dropped the other tooth in the evidence bag. Chain of evidence didn't mean a whole hell of a lot at this point. "Maybe if we took the teeth back to the ocean. Maybe."

"Big fucking maybe."

"You got a better idea?"

Mike took the teeth and stared at them. "Get Adam on the phone."

Ernie checked his notebook for the numbers Jeffries gave him. He dialed the number and listened. The voicemail picked up. Ernie hung up.

"No answer?"

Ernie shook his head.

"Didn't leave a message?"

"What the fuck am I supposed to say? This is the police, watch out for the ghost shark?"

"Point made." Mike stood up, dusted the seat of his pants off. "I guess we have to go do some actual police work." Mike offered Ernie a hand.

"Well, it was just a matter of time," he said as he got to his feet.

*****

Mike knocked on Adam's apartment door. They chose not to send uniforms ahead of them this time. The situation was getting harder and harder to explain and they figured they didn't have the time to do everything by the book.

The door opened a crack.

"Adam Stevens?"

"Yeah."

Mike tried to smile. "Detectives Paulson and Chambers, Boston PD, can we ask you a few questions?"

"They're dead, aren't they? Andrew and Pete, right? Fucking dead, right?"

Ernie and Mike shared a look. "Yeah," Ernie said. "You know anything about that?"

"Yeah," he said. "I know too much." He held out his fist through the crack of the door. No surprise, then, when he opened it to reveal a triangular, white shark tooth. It was bloody from where it had dug in his hand. He'd been holding it in a death grip.

"You need to come with us, sir," Mike said.

"I'm not leaving this apartment. I have a gun."

Mike glanced at Ernie. "Do you really think that will make a bit of difference?"

Adam blinked and then shut the door.

"Well, you're just a ray of sunshine," Ernie said.

Mike shrugged.

The door opened suddenly. Adam stood in front of them holding the shark tooth in one hand and a .44 Magnum in the other. "Let's go."

"Nice hand-cannon," Ernie said.

"Makes me less nervous," Adam said, staring at the gun.

Ernie gently removed the gun from the frantic man's hand. "Funny, it has the exact opposite effect on me."

They were quiet until they got to the car and were headed away. Mike spoke first. "You want to tell us what the hell is going on?"

"It's the fucking shark. The one we killed in Mexico. They never stop swimming, ya'know?"

"What's that?" Ernie turned around in the seat to look at the young man.

"They guy who took us out in his boat, Ortiz, he said that sharks never stop swimming. They have to keep moving or they drown."

"Sharks drown, huh?" Ernie glanced at Mike.

"Yeah." Adam shook his head like he didn't even believe what he was saying.

"You got that other tooth?" Ernie held up the bag with the other two teeth in it.

"What's that got to do with anything?"

"Where's the tooth?"

Adam struggled to open his shaking hand. "Here."

"This might actually work," Mike said.

The rear window exploded. Broken safety glass and saltwater showered the inside of the car.

Mike slammed forward into the steering wheel as the water hit the inside of the windshield, blinding him.

Ernie pulled his piece. "Stop the fucking car! Stop the fucking car!"

Adam screamed, his voice rising and falling like a siren.

Mike slammed the breaks on.

Crying, Adam crashed forward into the front seat. Blood spit out of his mouth.

"Go!" Ernie saw something glide behind the car illuminated by the red of the brake lights. "Go! Fucking go!"

Mike stomped the gas and the car shot down the dark, empty street.

"I'm bleeding," Adam said. "Oh God, Oh God. I'm really bleeding."

"Really?" Mike glanced back in the rear view mirror. "I think we lost it."

Ernie struggled to turn himself around in his seat. The floor was flooded with bloody water. Adam lay stretched out across the whole back seat, writhing. Mike swerved as he approached traffic, and Ernie smacked the back of his head against the inside of the car. "Slow down," he barked.

"No," Adam said. "Tiger shark, they can swim...something like...twenty miles an hour."

Mike looked in the mirror again. He thought he saw something move between two cars behind him, but he couldn't be sure. "I can't just drive around all night. What the fuck are we going to do?"

"We need to get to the ocean," Ernie said. He stuffed the last tooth in the evidence bag. We need to take this back and dump it in the water."

"Ancestor spirits," Adam said. "The guy in Mexico.

He said they hold the sharks sacred, something about their teeth."

"So you killed a *sacred* shark?"

"You fucked up real good, didn't you, Adam? Didn't you? You dumb shit."

Mike shot through traffic, cut off a semi and sped up an on-ramp. "Who wants to go to the beach?"

"We can't take you to a hospital. You understand that, right?" Ernie patted Adam on the shoulder.

He nodded. "Just...it'd just get me in a hospital bed." The kid was shaking, his eyes tearing up.

"Yeah."

"I'm scared. I'm fucking terrified."

"Me too," Ernie said, trying to keep pressure on the kid's wounds. It also helped to keep them covered, so he didn't see them.

"I told them to fucking forget the shark. Fucking Andrew had to do it. You could see it when he talked about it. Skydiving, swimming with the sharks, all the pussy one guy could handle and he has to shoot some fucking shark. I told him, I fucking told him...I..."

"Oh, shit," Mike said from the front seat. "Did he just die?"

Ernie felt for a pulse. "No, I think he just passed out. Yeah, he's still breathing."

"Not for long, though."

"I'm not a fucking doctor, Mike, Jesus."

"We have a suspect dying in the back seat of our car."

"He's not a fucking suspect."

"Okay, okay, okay, okay," Mike said, pounding on the steering wheel with the palm of his hand. He swerved across the interstate and shot down the ramp.

When he got to the docks, Mike was half-tempted to drive the car straight into the water, but he skidded to a halt.

The boats, mostly rusty wrecks, were piled up here like a child's bathtub toys, jumbled together in a heap. It made Ernie think of pictures he'd seen of that Japanese tsunami from a couple years ago. "What the hell, Mike? Eight-hundred miles of shoreline and you pick this?"

"Look," Mike said, remarkably calm considering the situation. "If this thing goes sideways..."

"*If?* If it goes sideways? This thing has gone so far sideways that it's practically come back on the other side."

"If this goes bad, we don't need bystanders."

"It's...it's coming! I can feel it."

Ernie nodded. "Let's do this."

Mike sprung from the driver's side of the car. Ernie tossed the evidence bag to Mike, who didn't break stride as he ran toward the nearest pier.

Ernie helped Adam out of the back seat. He was pale and shaky from blood loss.

Mike dashed out on the rickety platform. The wood gave way and he stumbled forward, dropping the teeth. They went over the side of the railing. Something hit the water.

He ran to the side and looked over.

One of the triangular shark teeth sat on top of a pylon, the other hung from the leather strap.

"Shit," Mike said. He hesitated for a second and then jumped into the water. He swam over to the pylon, grabbed the tooth and tossed it out to sea. "Two down one to go!"

"It's here," Adam said.

Ernie scanned the darkness at the edge of the lot. He saw nothing at first, but after a second he saw a movement in the shadows. "Shit." Drawing his piece, he moved between Adam and the shadow. The darkness swam toward them.

Ernie levelled his pistol and squeezed off a shot. He hit it dead-on, but it didn't even flinch. He fired again, but nothing changed.

Mike struggled in the water, but could not reach the hanging tooth. "Ernie!"

The shadow moved closer and the darkness had teeth.

Ernie turned away. From where he stood, he could see the hanging tooth. He brought his pistol up and fired.

The shot cut the strap and the tooth hit the water.

The shadow dissipated in the glare of the headlights.

Ernie slumped against the car.

Mike trudged up from the water. He removed his cigarettes, dumped out the seawater and put one in his mouth. "Aint that a bitch."

"You still alive, Adam?"

Adam groaned.

"Good enough for me," Mike said, calling it in. Minutes later, an ambulance screamed in the distance. "Ghost shark, huh?"

"I know, right?" Ernie patted Mike on the shoulder. "C'mon, I'll buy you some chili."

Ernie opened the car door, dumping several gallons of seawater onto the ground. He didn't even blink as he slid into the passenger seat. Mike sloshed into the driver's seat. Mike turned the car away from the ocean and headed back into Boston.

Last Minute

The two vampire kids appeared out of the swirling snow as Jim crossed the Best Buy parking lot headed back to his truck. Judging from their black clothes, crisscrossed with silver buckles and leather ties, Jim figured they had come straight from the Hot Topic. He hated last minute Christmas shopping, but Emma was still mad from him searching her room and he hoped that a little extra gift under the tree from Dad might smooth things over. Jacob, who was usually no problem at all, would benefit from Jim's parental guilt as well. If you couldn't buy your kid's love, Jim figured, what was the point?

"You'd better not pout. You'd better not cry," one said.

The two of them together were barely one-hundred pounds of pimply teenage boy-child, but they stood like they owned the place. Jim had to admit though, there was something unsettling about them. They were practically identical. "You guys look like you could be twins or something."

"Or something," the other one said. They both laughed.

"Enough," Jim said, stepping forward and pushing the one boy out of his way. The boy resisted, and for one icy moment, Jim felt like he was pushing against a steel pole, cold and immovable, but then the boy stepped aside and let Jim pass. He *let* me pass, Jim thought. "You emo kids are getting more aggressive every day."

"Emo? I remember when we were goth."

"I remember when we were Visigoth."

"Good times."

As Jim listened to the boys talk, it became increasingly difficult to tell who was talking or if either of them were. "Yeah, well, Merry Christmas," Jim said, heading back toward his truck. He felt his stride increase, until he was practically running. He slipped on some black ice and spun his arms to keep his balance. He stuffed his small shopping bag into his jacket and reached for his keys, but they weren't in his pocket. He checked the other coat pocket. He felt the square of his wallet and the smaller rectangle of his cell phone, but no keys.

The kids.

The kids were gone. They had been standing there a second ago. Jim scanned the empty parking lot. Except for the light post, he found himself alone in the dark and the snow. His footprints in the drifting snow ran in a more or less straight line back to the building. He didn't see the boy's footprints. Jim's brow furrowed. The snow, he thought, it drifted and covered the prints. He could still see his prints, though. Nervously scanning the parking lot, Jim hurried back toward the building looking on the ground for his keys.

"You lose something, mister," a voice said. One of the vampire kids stood just to one side. Jim could have sworn he hadn't been there a moment ago, but he had been looking down at the frozen ground.

"Huh? No. Yeah. I can't find my keys."

"That sucks," he said. He glanced around. "Did you look over there?" He pointed to a dark corner of the parking lot, unlit by the light post, where the ground sloped away to a large culvert, gaping darkness like a dragon's cave.

Jim stared at the culvert for longer than he meant to, but he was afraid that if he turned around and looked at the boy, he would see something that he did not want to see. "No," Jim said and swallowed. "I haven't been over there."

"Are you sure?"

"I don't think so."

"I could have sworn I saw you over there. If you want I'll go over there with you and help look."

Jim looked at the kid. He was smiling. His lips looked black in the blue winter night and ochre street light. There was nothing in this world that Jim wanted to do less than to go over to the darkness with this child. "You know what? Never mind. I'll just call Triple A and have them send out some help." Jim reached for his phone.

It was gone.

Trying not to panic, Jim patted his coat and jeans pockets. Nothing.

"You didn't lose your phone, did you?" The boy tilted his head and spoke very slowly, almost melodically. "Do you want me to help you look for it?"

"No, I can...I'm sure I can find it."

"Do you think it is over there?" The boy pointed an impossibly long finger in the direction of the dark culvert.

"I definitely didn't go over there." Jim's phone rang, startling him. He looked around on the ground, but even as it continued to ring, he did not see it.

"There it is," the boy said. Jim didn't have to look to know where he was pointing.

"Where's your friend?"

The boy shook his head. "I haven't got any friends."

The phone rang again and Jim could see it light up on the edge of the parking lot overlooking the dark culvert. The static of the snow kept him from seeing what might be in the concrete cylinder.

"Let's go get it, so we can call for help," the boy said walking in that direction.

Jim followed him, fists clenched at his sides.

"You out Christmas shopping?" He crouched in the snow and retrieved Jim's cell phone.

"Yeah," Jim said.

"Us too," the boy said. The other boy appeared out of the darkness behind him. He was holding Jim's truck keys. Beyond them, in the dark of the culvert, Jim could see red eyes watching him.

Jim took his shopping bag out of his pocket. "I have two Ipods for my kids. I have a family. Jacob...Emma...Susan..."

One of the boys took the bag, looked inside, and smiled. Fangs filled the boy's mouth.

"I have a family," Jim said.

"So do we," the other boy said. "And you know how family gatherings can be."

"I...I don't understand."

"Christmas dinner," the boy said.

The darkness moved. It had faces and hands and arms and teeth. Flat on his back, Jim could feel the cold of the pavement beneath him and the crushing weight on top of him. Sharp pains all over his body. He could hear the blood being drained from his body. "Emma," he said. "Jacob."

"I hate last minute Christmas shopping," the one boy said.

"Next year we start earlier."

"Agreed."

The Killing Jar

"I hate bugs," Sam said, shaking the empty mayonnaise jar with the toe of his sneaker. The insect inside rattled. Sam shivered with deep disgust. "Can we just go play some ball or something?"

Sam was the starting pitcher for the Junior High Rockets and any excuse to stretch his arm was good enough for him. This Saturday, though, he had no game, so he rode his bike down to Bobby's. He found the older boy in the shed behind his parent's trailer, mismanaging a box of empty baby food jars.

"I have to catch a few more specimens for my 4-H project. I'm running out of time," Bobby said. He carefully filled a backpack with baby food jars.

"You always wait 'till the last minute for your 4-H shit," Sam said, keeping a safe distance from Bobby's specimens. "4-H stands for head, heart, hot dogs and handjobs, right?"

"Exactly," Bobby said without looking up from what he was doing. "That's why your sister joined."

"I'd say 'screw you', if it wasn't the truth."

Both boys laughed.

"So what do you need to do?"

"Catch some bugs, kill some bugs, mount some bugs."

"I'm not touching that creepy crawly shit, dude," Sam said, nose wrinkled. "I'm sorry, but even in our friendship, I have to draw the line somewhere."

"Have you always been such a big pussy?"

Sam shrugged. "Pretty much."

"I don't need you to touch any bugs, princess. I just wanted you to go with me."

"Go where?"

"I just didn't want to go by myself. Boring, ya'know?"

"Yeah." Sam's curiosity was piqued. "Wait a second...where?"

Bobby sighed, looking up from his backpack. It was obvious that he was avoiding actually saying it. "Smith's Creek."

Sam held up his empty hands. "Uh, no thanks dude, Junior West said he saw lights down there. It's fucking creepy."

"It's not creepy and Junior sniffs model glue. He sees lights all the time."

"Fair point," Sam said. "But, dude, I don't know. The boys stared at each other for a minute, until Sam couldn't look in Bobby's blue pleading blue eyes any longer. "Alright, it's pretty bright out. Just a couple of hours, then."

"I appreciate it, man. I've found bugs down there that don't even live in Indiana. I need to find something awesome. I'll make a bug lover out of you yet."

"Fat chance."

*****

Sam and Bobby rode their bikes down to Smith Creek and ditched them in the bushes on the side of the dirt road.

While Bobby shrugged his backpack on to his shoulder, Sam stared into the darkness of the woods. The trees formed a nearly solid wall between where the boys stood and where they were headed.

Bobby joined Sam. "Is kinda creepy, huh?"

"Yeah." Sam sighed looking at Bobby. After a bit, he grinned. "So, what are you looking for, anyway?"

It seemed to break the tension. Bobby shrugged. "I don't know, really. Something exotic. Something I haven't seen before."

"Something you haven't seen before," Sam repeated, staring back at the trees. "Well, let's get to it, then." Sam ducked into the ditch, climbed the rusty wire fence and disappeared into the woods. Bobby followed close behind, careful not to jostle his backpack full of glass jars.

After they got past the wall of trees, the day was darker and cooler than it had been out on the road. Walking abreast, they fell into a comfortable rhythm.

"You going to ask Sara Price out?"

"Don't know. Doubt it."

"She likes you, ya'know?"

"Bullshit."

"No kidding, her sister told me."

"Tammy?"

"No, the other one, Cathy."

"Oh, *Cathy*."

"Why'd you say it like that?"

"Cathy told you that Sara likes me?"

"Yeah, so?"

"So, Cathy likes *you*. She knows you're my best friend. She probably just wanted something to talk to you about. I doubt that Sara even knows I exist."

"Cathy likes me?"

"Sometimes, I feel like I'm talking to myself." Sam stopped, held his hand up. "You hear that?"

"Yeah, you said you're talking to yourself."

"No, that...noise. Hear it?"

They stood in silence, heads cocked listening.

Bobby shook his head. "Don't hear it. Deer?"

"Don't think so." After a second, they continued walking.

"You trying to freak me out?"

"Yup. You scared, yet?"

"Terrified. You been sniffing glue?"

"Not me, I have asthma, I only sniff gas. I have been known to eat paste, though."

"That good peppermint-y kind from kindergarten? Good shit. I can't blame you."

A few more steps and they broke out of the trees and found themselves on the sandy bank of Smith's Creek. The water bubbled noisily around the rocks and around the snaking roots of a tree that was half-washed away by the running water. Sam stopped suddenly almost stumbling into the water. "Weird," he said.

"What?"

"Didn't hear the water until I almost stepped in it. Sort of snuck up on me."

Bobby nodded. "Yeah, weird, I guess. Dude, you okay?"

Sam laughed humorlessly, like he was trying too hard. "Just got the creeps, I guess. How do you kill the bugs you catch, anyway?"

"Killing jar," Bobby said, digging a different glass jar out of his backpack. Sam noticed that something was stuck to the bottom. "You put the bugs in with some poison, airtight and they just die in there. Humane, I guess."

"Only if you're not a bug, right?"

"I thought you hated bugs?"

Sam shrugged and then started down the bank of the creek. A dragonfly zoomed away from them like a little helicopter across the water. "Where do we start?"

"I'll show you," Bobby said. The boys spent the next hour turning over logs, searching tree branches and in the knee-high grass and ferns that covered the hollow that surrounded Smith's Creek.

Every once and awhile, Bobby would squat down pick something up and examine it.

Sometimes, Sam noticed, he greedily saved the specimen in a jar and sometimes he gently returned the insect to the ground. "Condom wrapper," he said, holding up a twist of green foil.

"Ribbed?"

"Wait...yup. How did you know?"

"I'm sensitive to a woman's needs." Sam squatted down on the bank of the creek watching what seemed like a thousand tadpoles swarm beneath the bubbling green water.

"See you know stuff like that. You should ask Sara out."

"I don't know about Sara, ya'know? Girls, man, I don't know. Do you ever feel like you just don't fit right with everybody else? I don't even know how to say it, dude. My parents wouldn't understand for a second, man. Bobby, ya'know? It's like, I see that Sara is pretty or whatever, but she just doesn't mean anything to me. Girls, like. Do you ever feel like that? Like girls or whatever just aren't the answer? Dude? Hello?" When he got no answer, Sam climbed the steep bank and headed toward where Bobby had been looking for specimens. "Dude? Are you even listening to me? I..."

The man was holding Bobby by the neck. Bobby's feet were dangling, not even touching the ground. He had ahold of the man's hands, trying to pry them off of him.

"Hey," Sam said, running toward them. "Get the fuck off of him!"

At the sound of Sam's voice, the man turned toward him. At first, Sam thought the man was wearing some kind of motorcycle helmet his head was so big. It reflected metallic green in the muted light beneath the trees, like the bodies of blow flies that swarmed on road kill.

The man's antennae wriggled on top of his head as his mandibles opened and closed. Yellow eyes regarded Sam from top of his massive insectoid head. With his free hand, he reached for Sam.

Sam ran.

He stumbled across the creek, splashing as he stumbled. He fell down, sucking in a mouthful of muddy water and scrambled onto the bank and up the side of the hollow. He didn't stop running until he got back to the wire fence and could barely make it back over.

"Help," he said, still coughing creek water. He vomited in the grass as soon as he managed to get over the fence. Sam grabbed his bike and stood it up. He'd get help. He had to find someone to help.

Sam looked down at Bobby's bike where it lay in the grass. He wiped the vomit from his mouth with the back of his bare arm. "Shit. Shit. Shit." Sam climbed back over the fence and headed into the woods as quickly and quietly as he could.

*****

Sam peeked over the edge of the creek bank. The creature was just standing there, holding Bobby.

Sam grabbed a rock out of the creek bed. Smooth and round, it felt heavy in his hand. He wound up and let it fly as hard and as fast as he could, a perfect curveball above and to the right of the strike zone.

It hit the bug man square in the head. He stumbled forward, but did not release Bobby.

"Shit," Sam said, ducking down into the tall grass and weeds at the edge of the creek. His head was down low, his face almost in the water. He didn't think the thing had seen him, but he didn't know too much about bugs and with those multi-faceted eyes it could see a complete three-sixty for all Sam knew.

The thought had only just occurred to him, but he wished he had his dad's rifle. The bug man's what-do-you-call-it, *exoskeleton,* looked pretty solid and he didn't even know if a bullet would crack that shell. He grabbed another stone from the creek. Didn't really matter, didn't have a gun anyway, he thought.

Something seized him by the back of his neck and lifted his clean off his feet. Water and mud dripped from his body.

The bug man stared at Sam. It tilted its head and examined him. Its antennae danced at the top of its triangular head, mandibles vibrating.

The creature held Sam up to his face, turning him one way and then the other, looking him over like Sam might do if he caught too small a fish.

He's trying to decide whether to keep me or throw me back. "Let me go!" Sam kicked his feet.

The bug man shook Sam violently. A sound escaped the creature like the sound of a fax machine over the telephone. He could only imagine what he was saying, but he stopped kicking.

He lifted Sam up and with his free hand removed a small device from his belt. He held it up to Sam's body.

Measuring me, Sam thought.

From the higher vantage point, Sam could see Bobby trapped in a clear container several yards away. Bobby was pounding his fists against the inside of the clear box.

Sam knew what it was instantly. A killing jar. Bobby was a specimen.

"Fuck you!" Sam drew back the other stone and whipped in the bug man's face. It reeled back, dropping Sam and clutching at its ruined eye.

Sam hit the ground, tumbled in the dirt and got to his feet. He was running before the bug man could recover.

He dashed to the box and struggled with what looked like the handle, but it didn't budge.

Sam scrambled around looking for something to break the glass. Some of the bug man's tools were spread out on the grass. Sam grabbed one with a sharp point and swung it against the box.

It bounced off.

The material looked like glass, but it was like striking a steel plate.

Bobby's face was turning purple. His hand slapped against the glass slower now.

"Shit, shit, shit," Sam said, turning the strange tool around in his hands. If he could only make it work.

He drew it back and with all his strength slammed it against the latch, but nothing happened.

Sam hit it again and again.

Nothing.

Sam struck the tool against the box one last time and it buzzed to life, the sharp edge vibrating. Sam smiled. "Yeah!"

Something grabbed him around the waist. Looking down, Sam could see the bug man's pincered arms wrapped around his body. It squeezed the breath out of him.

Sam stabbed the tool into the thing's arm. It bit deep into the exoskeleton, slicing the arm and splattering blood.

The thing released him.

Sam wanted nothing more than to stick the tool between the thing's bulging yellow eyes, but he had more important things to do at the moment.

He slammed the tool against the killing box's locking mechanism and it sparked metal on metal. The latch broke and the lid popped open with a hiss of escaping gas. The smell made Sam dizzy and sick.

Bobby wasn't moving.

Sam dropped the tool and with both hands pulled Bobby free of the box. The two boys collapsed in the grass.

Bobby didn't seem like he was breathing.

Sam looked at the bug man, who still lay on the ground cradling his wounded arm.

Sam returned his attention to Bobby. He wished he knew how to do CPR. "Wait," Sam said, pulling his asthma inhaler out of the pocket of his jeans. The pushed the nozzle end of the gray plastic inhaler between the other boy's lips and sprayed. The medicine hissed into his mouth, but nothing happened.

Sam put his ear to Bobby's chest. "Please, oh please, oh please..."

Bobby's chest moved. He *was* breathing.

He wished again that he knew how to do CPR. Copying what he had seen in movies and on TV, he squatted next to Bobby's body, put both hands together on his chest and pushed down. He repeated this over and over again.

Bobby coughed suddenly, a wet bark.

Thank God, Sam thought. Sam looked to see if the bug man was still lying in the grass, but he was gone.

Shit. He could be anywhere. Sam scanned the forest.

Bobby coughed again.

"Got to be quiet, man, we have to get out of here," Sam said, trying to get Bobby to his feet. They hurried back through the woods. Sam kept looking over his shoulder.

Sam helped Bobby over the fence, but by the time they actually got to their bikes Bobby was on his feet and reasonably steady. He collapsed on the ground, but it took Sam a minute to realize that he was crying.

"It's okay man, I got you out of there. Everything is okay."

"You didn't see," Bobby said.

"I saw it was a killing jar, just like you told me."

"You didn't see."

"Didn't see what?"

"There were more killing jars. A lot more."

Together, the two boys stared at the forest. In the distance, they heard the cricket call of the bug man and after a few seconds it was answered and then again and again. Dozens of voices growing louder. Moving closer   .

Speaking Of Monsters

Professor Casket rarely revealed to anyone that he was not, in fact, a professor and never revealed that his surname was not actually Casket. He had done both in the first hour that he had spent with the man named Baron in the vampire pub, the Thirsty Bat, and he only had himself to blame. The man made his palms sweat and his eye twitch and only his money and the promise of more of it, calmed the Professor's nerves. He fondled the purse on the table in front of him.

The Thirsty Bat had once been a slaughter house and the rusty hooks that bled carcasses still hung from the ceiling. The bar dominated one wall and several tables crowded the small stone space. There were no windows, which seemed proper all around.

Despite his storied past as a bit of a monster hunter, James Casket did not feel that he was necessarily built for combat. Instead, he was tall and thin in his long leather coat and top hat. He had found himself in the right place at the right time on a number of occasions where monsters were involved and occasionally he was holding a blade or a crucifix. He considered himself the luckiest fool that had ever faced a werewolf or zombie.

Professor Casket had first come to know Baron through an acquaintance of an acquaintance and with this tentative introduction, he chose to meet him in London's submersible district where man and machine merged in more ways than one and business of varied and various forms went unnoticed. Baron lumbered down the winding backstreets, explaining that he had been hurt in the war and that much of him had been replaced mechanically.

"Baron," the man had said by way of introduction and seemed to feel no need to elaborate on either his royal status or his fertility. Baron was part man part machine, though it was impossible to determine what function he could possibly have served with his cumbersome mechanical arm and leg. One photomechanical eye flickered in his left socket, wheeling and focusing of its own accord.

Gretch, the undead waitress, appeared, quite literally, beside their corner table. "Who's your friend, Prof?" The vampire wench drifted past with a silver tray of bloodstained goblets. "Does he care to order a drink, or to become one?" A touch of vampire glamour in his eye added a dark spark to her single entendre.

"*Move along, my lovely,*" Casket said, he often felt flushed when he spoke in the vampiric tongue as if his very blood seemed to know what he was saying and did not care for it one bit.

Gretch's glorious mounds peaked out from beneath her leather bustier. Casket had fallen willing victim to her fangs and bosom on a number of occasions. Casket winked at her and she smiled a fanged grin in return. "Smooth talker, he is, a regular cunning linguist."

"Not a proper professor then, eh? Had me doubts in regards to your credentials anyway. Can talk to monsters well enough, I can see that with me own good eye. That's what I'm paying for."

"As advertised," Casket said, producing one of his dog-eared business cards (PROFESSOR JAMES CASKET PHANTASMAGORICAL LINGUIST---LYCAN, VAMPIRIC, ETC...) with a sleight of hand that impressed most of his clients, though, not as it turned out, Mr. Baron. "I explained to the proprietor that you're looking for your father..."

"Me old man, see, went off and happily got himself bitten by a lady bloodsucker that looked like a school girl, but was old enough to be his great gran. All well and good, I says, but me sick old mum wants to see him one last time before she goes on to be with the Lord." He crossed himself then, though improperly. "Don't even know if he'll understand a word I say," he added, lifting the dirty cup of whiskey to his lips.

"Don't," Casket said, putting his hand flat over the mouth of the glass. "Blood on your glass."

Baron nodded once and returned the glass to the table. He produced a silver flask from his great coat and tipped it toward Casket.

An awkward silence settled down between the two men.

Casket's mind slipped to the most recent night he had spent with Gretch in her cozy sepulcher. There was something life-affirming, he imagined, about making love in a silk-lined coffin. He rolled off the woman, fighting to catch his breath. She could easily be the death of him with either her fangs or her sex.

"Could turn you right now," Gretch had said, her fingers walking up his chest like a pale spider. "Be nothing at all, really." Gretch worked hard to give the façade of nonchalance, though Casket suspected that it was just that, a façade. She wanted nothing more than to make him like her and, after so many years, Casket had begun to suspect that he yearned for it, too. "You love me, don't you?"

Her vulnerability made him sigh. No living girl had set his heart racing like this exquisite corpse. "Not a question of love, my dear, but rather one of money."

"Same thing," she said, teasing him.

He did not like the idea of her selling herself, whether it be for blood or for gold. Those days were long in the past and, to be fair, Casket could not afford to take the high road, as some of the coins in her whore's purse were his.

The prospect of living forever tickled him, though the prospect of living forever with no money did not. Eternal poverty was not his notion of proper immortality. Vampires could not hope to make an honest living in England. Casket knew he would have to accumulate a small fortune if he hope to make a go of being a vampire. These days, even blood was not free.

"I know what you're thinking," Gretch said, squeezing his manhood.

"And now you're a mind-reader," he said, crawling on top of her.

In the pub, Casket could not help but smile.

"I'm happy to say that with a little, uh, excavation, I have been able to locate your father," Casket said, gesturing to the barkeep, who nodded back at him and then directed one of the vampires at the bar toward their table.

Hunched and skeletal, the man looked too old to live forever, looking as if he'd already lived several centuries the hard way. The old man took a seat with a slowness that was uncomfortable to watch.

"You've been...looking for me, Mr....Casket?"

"*Professor*, actually, Yes, on behalf of your son," he said, nodding toward Baron.

The old vampire looked as if he could not decide whether or not to laugh at this joke and chose, at last, not to. "This man is not my son!"

"Don't say that, father," Baron said, springing from his seat. The wooden stake in his meaty paw appeared, a feat of sleight of hand that put Casket's own to shame and disappeared into the elderly vampire's heart as quickly as it had appeared.

The elderly vampire collapsed in a pile of dusty bones and funeral rags.

Baron stood up, any sign of his limp gone with his pretense. His cane revealed a vicious blade that he quickly employed to behead the nearest bar patron whose blood splattered icy across Casket's face. Casket could not even scream as the head rolled across the floor.

Baron moved with the graceless power of a locomotive. He snapped the lid from his flask and doused another vampire with what was surely holy water. Screams and steam raced to the ceiling as it clutched at its face, melting away like candle wax.

He held open his mechanical hand and a silver crucifix sprang forth. Gretchen reeled away from it. With her back turned, she could not hope to see the blade cutting down on her.

Casket leapt between Baron and Gretch. "No!"

"Move, Professor," Baron said with a sickening calm.

"Never."

As quickly as a coal mine explosion, the attack ended and the pub was empty.

Sniffing, Baron re-sheathed his sword, produced a pair of pliers and went about the grisly business of removing the fangs from each fallen vampire.

Casket murmured something.

"What's that, Professor?"

"In...in God's name, why?"

"In God's name indeed," Baron said, looking around. "Church says I'm a step closer to heaven with each fang I take," he said, shaking the teeth in his palm like a gambler might do a pair of dice, but with a smile suggesting he had already won.

"They were...harmless."

He smiled a broader smile. "Good thing, too. These contraptions aren't cheap and I'd hate to see them ruined."

"You...murdered them."

"Obviously not a professor of law, then are you? Queen and Country say you can't murder a dead man." Baron picked up a skull and pried the fangs loose. He dropped the skull to the floor like you might drop an apple core when you had finished with the fruit. "Besides, you could have stopped me."

"I couldn't..."

"You could have. I asked around about you, Casket. Some big time monster hunter in your day, before you started chasing the dragon, eh? S'posed to help VanHelsing with that bloody Count Dracula business, but you were laid up in an opium den. Had to sell your silver bullets to pay your tab 'fore the whores would let your leave the premises. You could have stopped me."

Behind his back, Casket slid the blade out of his sleeve. He gripped the handle in his shaking hand.

Baron leaned forward. "You bought my story because you chose to. You were bought and paid for before we ever stepped foot in this place. He pushed himself nose to nose with Casket. "You did nothing..."

Casket tensed, finding his footing.

"...because you are nothing..."

Casket swallowed hard, finding with his eye the spot on Baron's thick neck.

"...nothing but talk." Baron reached across the table and took back the money. "Tell me, Professor, how exactly do you say *bugger yourself* in vampire talk?"

Casket's eyes focused on Baron's neck, but he couldn't move. His teeth clenched. He wanted nothing more than to leap and slash the man's jugular.

Baron stood up and, after a moment, left the pub. Casket dropped the blade, jumping as it stuck into the floor at his feet.

"What...have...you...done?" Gretchen's voice sounded like breaking glass.

Casket fell to the floor by her side, steadying her as she tried to stand. Her eyes bled from the sight of the cross. She pulled away from him. Struck out at him.

"Please," Casket said, still trying to help her even as her claws drew blood through the sleeve of his coat. "Please."

"You brought that madman here?"

"I thought...," he said, but could not continue. What had he thought? That Baron had been seeking his long lost father? Had he actually believed that rubbish? Casket could not stop shaking. "I needed the money, dear, for us...for our eternity..."

Gretch's tears washed the blood from her eyes. She spun toward Casket in anger. "I should kill you. I should take their blood out of you!"

"I would not even try to stop you," he said.

"No," Gretchen said. "You wouldn't, would you?" She shook her head and turned away from him. She swept out of the pub. "Don't look for me, James, you won't find me."

Casket fell into his chair. Hand shaking, he took the dirty cup of whiskey and drank it down. It burned his throat and tasted faintly of blood.

Hide Nor Hair

Dirig made no sound as he moved through the winter woods. The long, black duster he wore did not rustle as he slipped between frozen trees, nor did his big, old pistols rattle in their holsters. Only his thick boots left any evidence of his passing, heavy prints in the ice-glazed snow.

"We still get paid if we kill the wolf in human form?" Maclvoy had stopped to relieve himself and had begun to wonder. He was a professional soldier, a mercenary, fresh from security work in the Middle East and he saw everything, including werewolves, in dollars and cents. He saw hunting lycanthropes as a means to a wealthy end. Generally speaking, violence, no matter who it was administered on, paid well. Killing werewolves was legal, lucrative and generally encouraged by the general populace, not that public opinion usually bothered Maclvoy much, but, and he would not admit it to anyone, he did like playing the hero. He was like Beowulf with a machine gun.

Banks, busy catching snowflakes in the palm of his black leather gloves, stopped suddenly. "That is the stupidest thing I ever heard."

Maclvoy zipped up. "Why?"

"We just going to show up with some John Q. Public's head in a bag like he Lon Chaney Jr. or some shit? How they know we didn't just cap some pedestrian over his half-caf vanilla latte?"

Banks, on the other hand, was about accuracy. As a *street sweeper*, a hired gun for urban gangs, a man's worth was calculated not by how many men he'd killed, but by the colors of the men that had gone down. Bloods and Crips, it was all the same, but a man could not forget who was paying the bills, calling the shots this week. Banks had gotten tired of shooting brothers and statistics said that werewolves were more than ninety-percent Caucasian. Very few werewolves in Compton.

Maclvoy shrugged. "Mark of the beast?"

"Mark of the beast?"

"Yeah."

"That is the second stupidest thing I ever heard."

Maclvoy slung is rifle over his shoulder to free up his hands. When he was trying to explain something, he always talked with his hands. "Way I got it figured, your average werewolf is human most of the time, right?"

"Guess so."

"So odds are we're going to find Fido on two legs, not four."

Banks stood, holding his shotgun in both arms like he was cradling a child. "I concede your point."

"Really?"

"Naw," Banks said," but nothing scarier than a cracker with a machine gun and an idea."

They both laughed and turned to follow Dirig.

He had materialized in front of them, looking like he had begun to reconsider taking on two new assistants. He thoughtfully rubbed his gray goatee with one gloved hand. "We're already dead," he said. "We just haven't been made aware of the fact. The wolf, you see, is the messenger that makes us aware."

Banks and Maclvoy glanced at each other and then back to Dirig. After a moment of silence, it was Banks who spoke first. "I don't, uh, what do you mean?"

Dirig sighed. "Quit the chatter and march double time." He turned and stomped away, leaving his humongous footprints behind him.

Maclvoy rolled his eyes. "He was in *the war*," he finally said when he had estimated that Dirig was out of ear shot.

"Big whoop." Banks made a jerk-off gesture. "Which war?"

Maclvoy shrugged. "I dunno, Civil War?"

Chuckling, they hurried to catch up with Dirig.

There were no other legends in the hunt. Few got to try more than once to take down a werewolf. Of course, there were men who'd lost family to the beasts, who with a little luck and a lot of money had managed to not get killed and maybe put a few silver bullets into something out into the woods. No one had brought back carcasses. For all the werewolf remains that had been returned, there wasn't enough to reconstruct one full werewolf. Some brought out Gray Wolves or wild dogs and hunted the others to near extinction.

That was before Dirig.

Bleeding near to death, Dirig dragged the remains of a werewolf he'd killed out of the Rocky Mountains. He had killed the thing with a silver knife that had more in common with a medieval sword than your average piece of cutlery.

Dirig had killed so many werewolves in his career that it caused one man to remark that Dirig didn't go out to kill them but rather they came to him to die.

Very little was known of Dirig and the general consensus was that was a good thing. What he had seen, what he had done would, hopefully, die with him after the last werewolf.

The men kept to the more traveled hiking paths, following the sun as it settled into the western sky. The color of the snow and the light had shifted from blinding white to a cold blue, by the time they found the first body.

"All I'm saying," Banks whispered. "I'm a professional killer, son, *pro*-fessional. I don't need any of his Sun-Tzu, hut-two-three-four bullshit..."

Dirig stopped, holding one fist up above his head.

The two men stopped, shouldering their weapons and turning in slow circles, scanning the icy wall of pine trees that surrounded them. They had not noticed how tight the path had gotten, how close the trees were. Something could explode from this cover and take them both before they had the chance to properly shit themselves.

Dirig crouched down next to where the snow was a thick maroon. He dipped his fingers in the blood.

"If he licks that shit' I'm gonna puke," Banks said.

Dirig wiped it on his boots, stood up and gestured that they should continue.

The men followed, rubber-necking at the kill like it was a particularly grisly car wreck on their morning commute. To them, it was: Pedestrian vs. werewolf.

The dead woman, blond and dressed in an immaculately white ski suit, lay in such a pile that she did look like 'he'd been hit by a truck. Her skin had already turned blue, giving her the appearance of a broken doll. It made Banks think of his Gramma Nana's Hummel figurines. "Monsters always kill the pretty ones," he said as they passed. "Never the ugly bitches."

Maclvoy shook his head, gesturing to a sign that indicated that this was a difficult hiking path.

"No shit," Banks said.

"We make camp here," Dirig said.

"Great," Maclvoy said, shrugging off his pack. "I was hoping to sleep next to a beautiful woman tonight."

*****

When they had made camp and gotten a decent fire going, Maclvoy found himself drawn back to the kill.

"You leave that poor girl alone," Banks said. "She's had a rough day."

"Dirig," Maclvoy said, feeling odd saying the man's name. "I think I found something...shit...I found something." He held up a Spongebob Squarepants ski-hat.

Dirig took it. "Well, that wasn't hers. Where did you find it?"

Maclvoy showed him. After a frenzied moment of digging with his gloved hand, he found more. "All these clothes. Bloody. Looks like a whole family. Two or three maybe."

"Damn," Banks said. "Just dragged everybody off?"

"Why leave Mommy, then?"

Banks stood up straight, squinting into the darkness. "Maybe he was planning on coming back."

Dirig said nothing.

"Keep your backs to the fire, saves your night vision," Maclvoy said as the three men headed back to the camp.

"Aint you a good soldier," Banks said.

Maclvoy laughed. "Fuck you, gangbanger."

Dirig disappeared into his tent, leaving the two men on watch. They settled, back to back on either side of the fire. Banks cleared his throat. "You notice Dirig's tracks?"

"You'd have to be blind to miss them."

"He added blood."

"Smell him coming a mile away."

"Like he wants to be tracked."

"Yeah."

"Maclvoy?"

"Yeah?"

"You wonder what happened to his other assistants."

"I prefer to think they are currently enjoying an early retirement someplace warm and werewolf free."

"Yeah," Banks said. "That isn't what I was thinking." He sat quietly for a minute. "When the shit goes down?"

"Yeah?"

"I got your back."

"Good to know," Maclvoy said, "but this aint any *Brokeback Mountain* shit, is it?"

Banks laughed. "Cracker, you aint even my type."

"My booty aint big enough ?"

"Much love to the sisters," Banks said. "You ought to try you one on, whitebread, you might change your whole perspective."

"Why, do *you* have a sister?"

"Hey, now."

"I like blonds, personally," Maclvoy said. "First girl I ever kissed was a blond."

"That's sweet," Banks said. "You sniff your finger afterwards?"

"Thanks, for ruining that memory for me."

"So Mommy over there *is* your type, huh?"

"I like 'em a little warmer, but yeah, there was something about her. She must have been fine when she was alive."

"Shit," Banks said, springing to his feet. His tone had changed.

"What, man?" Maclvoy scrambled to stand, but found his leg was asleep.

"Mommy's gone."

Stunned, the two men stared at the bloody patch of snow, not ten feet away from where they had been sitting.

"Better tell the old man," Maclvoy said, backing away from the fire.

Dirig's tent sat empty.

"Aw, shit," Banks said. "Now, where the hell did he go?"

"How the fuck should I know?" Inside the dark tent, Maclvoy spotted something. "Well, he couldn't have gotten too far without his boots." Maclvoy slung his rifle and snatched up Dirig's enormous boots. They still had blood on them. "You don't think something...got him, do you?"

"Dirig? King Swaggercock Werewolf Hunter? Doubt it."

"What then?"

'He's been leaving a trail with those giant shitkickers of his since we got out here."

"Leading them to him."

"Him? Try again, son. He aint here. It's us."

"I guess we know what happened to the other assistants."

Banks nodded. "Served up as dog food. We're fucking bait."

Somewhere a frozen branch snapped, startling both men. It could have easily been a thin bough cracking under the weight of so much ice and accumulated snow, but as Maclvoy and Banks stared at each other, they knew that it wasn't

Banks shouldered his shotgun and Maclvoy snapped the safety off on his rifle. "Whatever comes out of the woods," Maclvoy said, aiming at the treeline.

"Damn straight," Banks said. "Damn straight."

A limb bounced, dropping a soft mound of snow to the ground. It made to noise when it hit.

Banks tensed.

Beneath his breath, Maclvoy chanted, "Oh, shit. Oh, shit. Oh, shit."

The boy could not have been older than ten. Shaking with cold and terror, he stumbled naked from the embrace of the black branches. Blood dripped from his face and hands. He managed an uncertain step and collapsed.

"Take this," Maclvoy handed his rifle to Banks and hurried to the fallen child.

"Man, I 'don't know...," Banks said.

"The wolf attacked the family, dragged them off, he survived." Maclvoy took his coat off and wrapped the boy with it as he lifted him up. "You got a first aid kit?"

"Fuck no, I 'don't," Banks said, dropping the weapons. He fumbled in the backpacks piled by the fire. "I shoot shit, I 'don't bandage shit."

"This kid is going to bleed to death before you..."

"Here go," Banks said, holding up the first aid kit. White box, red cross.

"Not his blood..."

The boy sunk his teeth into Maclvoy's arm.

Maclvoy howled.

"Oh, shit," Banks screamed, dropping the first aid kit and lunging for the guns.

The boy unfolded in muscle and bone, snout punching out of his face, canines piercing deeper into Maclvoy's arm.

"Oh, God! Oh, God! Oh, God!" Maclvoy frantically pulled at his arm, trying to free it from the wolf's maw. "Shoot it! Shoot it!"

Banks tried to aim, but the wolf twisted Maclvoy in between the two of them and began backing into the woods."

Maclvoy clawed at the ground, trying to stop himself, but found only snow and frozen earth. "Shoot it!"

Banks fired, but at the last second something slammed into him, knocking him to the ground. He grabbed the shotgun and managed to rack a shell in before a massive weight dropped on his back. He heard a cracking sound that might have been his ribs.

A growl shook Bank's whole body.

Banks rammed the shotgun over his shoulder and pulled the trigger.

Falling away, the wolf howled.

Banks rolled over onto his back, pumping another shell into the shotgun and fired into the stunned wolf's face. "Fuck yeah! Silver shot, bitch!"

He got to his feet, racking the shotgun. The werewolf lay sprawled on the ground. "Two of them, goddammit." Banks rammed the shotgun into the wolf's ear and pulled the trigger. He stumbled back, trying to catch his breath. *Maclvoy.* "Where you at, cracker?"

Maclvoy screamed, a distant muffled sound.

Banks raced into the woods, grabbing Maclvoy's rifle as he went.

*****

Dirig crouched in the dark woods just outside the clearing. He knew from past experience that if he remained still, he all but vanished. His breathing had slowed to the point where he doubted that even the wolves could hear him.

Barefoot, he moved into the clearing, and descended on the dead werewolf. It had not been a good kill. Messy. Banks had led his whole chance of survival boil down to what amounted to a coin toss. An older wolf would have bitten the back of his head open before he got his hands on the shotgun. This one was a puppy, at best.

Dirig scooped up the beast's insides and slathered them on himself. Once, a long time ago, the smell had been ungodly, now though, Dirig hardly noticed. When he was covered, he drew his long silver knife from its sheath and went into the woods the way Banks had gone.

*****

Banks had begun to miss pavement in a real and meaningful way. He would have happily paid ten-grand for a streetlight as he bounded into the woods. He slung Maclvoy's rifle in favor of his own shotgun. It took him precious seconds to find his flashlight, but as soon as he flicked it on, the wolf's eyes sparkled at the end of the beam. Maclvoy's steaming blood looked black on the blue-white snow.

Even as Banks took hurried aim, the wolf's snout was buried in the bloody mess of Maclvoy's shoulder. "Bitch!"

The wolf darted out of the beam and disappeared into the base of a thirty-foot pine. Banks fired at the thing, but he doubted that he hit anything. Smoking pine needles and snow sparkled in the harsh beam of light.

"You can't shoot shit," Maclvoy said, struggling to speak around a bubbling mouthful of blood.

"I got one dog-face already. How many you got?"

Maclvoy made a weak gesture toward where the wolf had vanished. "I almost had him before you scared him off."

"Well, shit," Banks said, trying to get his arm under Maclvoy's armpit. "I can come back later if you're busy."

Maclvoy's chuckled cracked into a sob. "Fucking kid ate my arm."

"Hope that wasn't your pleasuring hand."

Maclvoy tried to laugh, but could only cough. "Two dogs?"

"Yeah, two little ones, Dick and Jane, must be the kids."

"Oh, shit," Maclvoy said. "Two kids."

"What?"

"That family..."

"Shit, shit, shit. That family wasn't victims..."

"No."

"We got to get gone," Banks said, heading back toward the campfire. He knew it wasn't the smartest idea, but his mind was blank and it seemed better than standing in the dark waiting to die. It was a full day's hike from where they'd started and there was no way Banks could drag Maclvoy that far and fight off a family, a pack, a whole fucking pack, of werewolves.

"Son-of-a-bitch, Dirig," Maclvoy said.

"Gonna cut off his head and shit down his neck."

Banks and Maclvoy broke through to the campsite. "Can't go on," Maclvoy said.

Banks stopped. "C'mon, you gotta take my sister out."

Maclvoy laughed. "She look like you?"

Banks gently lowered him to the ground. "Nowhere near as pretty as me."

"Poor girl."

Banks had never seen so much blood come out of one body. Maclvoy looked almost transparent. "I don't know what to do."

"Run like hell, man." Maclvoy died bad.

"Aw, hell no," Banks said, struggling to his feet. He wiped snot off his face with the sleeve of his coat. "Son-of-a-bitch!"

Banks took Maclvoy's rifle, slung it over his neck so that he could fire it with one hand and held the shotgun in the other. The kickback would probably knock him on his ass. Didn't matter. Banks took three steps before the first wolf appeared at the edge of the camp. Even on all fours, it still towered over him.

Banks tensed his fingers on the triggers. Another wolf appeared at his periphery. This one was impossibly taller.

Clouds of his frozen breath came out so fast that his head looked like it might be on fire.

Behind him, he could hear the softer footfalls of the smaller wolf, the boy.

The largest wolf sniffed at the remains of Bank's first kill. The wolf growled, rumbling the ground.

"Sorry, yo, but that bitch had to be put down."

The wolves rushed him, canines bared.

Screaming, Banks pulled both triggers.

*****

Dirig crouched just beyond the edge of the clearing and watched Banks die. When the wolves began to feed, when their muzzles were so buried inside Bank's body cavity that their eyes were partially covered with meat, Dirig casually stepped up to them, drew both pistols and put silver bullets into their brains.

The carcasses flopped to the ground.

Dirig turned slowly and locked eyes with the younger wolf, the boy. Dirig holstered his two pistols and slowly unsheathed his silver knife.

The young werewolf bolted.

After a few seconds, Dirig followed.

Dirig tracked the boy until the sky in the East began to lighten. He found the boy curled up and shivering in the fetal position. Young werewolves sometimes struggled to keep their bestial forms. He nearly passed the boy, concealed as he was by the nearly knee-high snow. Dirig lifted the boy by the scruff of the neck and carried him back to the camp. He wrapped him in a wool Army blanket and set him by the fire. "Hungry?"

The boy could not meet his eyes. He shook his head once.

"No," Dirig said, sitting on a stone by the dying fire. He glance at MacIvoy's half-devoured corpse, a bloody heap on the edge of the wood line. "Guess you wouldn't be, would ya?"

"What now?" The boy wiped at the dried blood that painted a five o'clock shadow on his prepubescent face.

Dirig removed one of his large pistols and cocked back the hammer. He rested the big gun on his leg. He squinted at the boy in the morning's gray half-light. "I suppose we'll wait."

The boy's eyes dropped to the ground. "For what?"

"The messenger," Dirig said. "We'll wait right here for the wolf to return."

The Night Men Running

Jeremiah ran from the dead men as fast as his withered leg would allow. The night air clawed at his lungs and his heart beat against his chest like the marching drum. Jeremiah ran like the whole Union army was bearing down on him.

Born a cripple, Jeremiah had not run much in his sixteen years. He had not run when the cruel older children chased him, beat him for being worthless. He had not run when the Union army had broken through his regiment's line and sent them running. He had hidden, instead, among the corpses until he could hobble back to his own men.

He ran now, though, because the dead men had made promises to him. They promised him an ugly death for his betrayal and though he feared death as much as any sane man, it was what might come after that filled his hammering heart with terror.

Days before, he had staggered into camp to discover his decimated regiment cowering in the muddy tents, clutching their rifles and staring into the gray morning dark. The camp had been made in the shadow of a two-story stone building with a church roof. The men appeared out of the mist like ghosts. All at once, they snapped their rifles towards him and he thought he would survive the Union army to die at the hands of his own side.

"Cripple," someone said.

The rifles sank back down.

The Union regiment that has so destroyed them were known as the Mad Dogs, on account of their charging into each skirmish barking and howling like lunatics. Even after identifying himself to the men, Jeremiah could still guarantee himself a deadly rain of ball slugs with as much as a simple growl. The men were a lit cannon fuse and it was just a matter of time before they found a reason to blow.

A scream ripped across the morning, but the assembled men did not even flinch. They knew where the scream came from and they chose to ignore it.

Exhausted, Jeremiah followed the man's cries through the chaotic maze of makeshift tents until he found the place where the mud was maroon with blood.

"Hold his legs, boy," Doctor Dubois said, saw in hand. His tone was frighteningly calm considering he was halfway through a femur when Jeremiah appeared at the clearing.

"No, please," Lieutenant Danner said, practically unintelligible around the piece of tree branch clamped in his teeth. Jeremiah understood. He knew what words were said when the saw came. They all said the same things. They all begged and prayed and cried. Jeremiah figured that if the saw ever came for him he have some of the same words to say. Jeremiah seized the man's flailing leg and leaned all of his weight upon it.

Whey the were finished and what was left of the good Lieutenant was taken to the recovery tent, where the men cradled missing limps and stared into nothing, Dr. Dubois led Jeremiah back to his tent and allowed the boy to watch as he slowly anesthetize himself into his usual post-surgical stupor.

"Where are we? I saw a building. A church?"

"School," the Doctor said, raking his fingers through the tangle of white hair on his head. "Girl's school.

Retreating and Captain Benning found this school. Thought the Union army would take *liberties* with the girls if we left them here unguarded." Doctor Dubois shook his head gently as if he doubted his own words.

"Captain Benning is a good man," Jeremiah said. Benning had once let Jeremiah carry ammunition during a minor skirmish and afterward the Captain called him a hero of the Confederacy. Sometimes, when it was quiet and dull, Jeremiah imagined that Captain Benning was actually his father. His own father had been a bastard and Jeremiah had difficulty conjuring an image of the man's face in his memory.

"Benning is an idiot," the Doctor said. "He sleeps in a warm bed, eats hot meals and probably takes his own liberties..."

"I sure am bushed, Doc." Jeremiah had no interest in hearing Dubois disparage the Captain.

Dubois huffed. "Dismissed."

Jeremiah curled up in the corner of one of the empty tents and slept. He thought, in the darkest hour of the night, that he heard the sound of men running, but it drained down into a dream of running black horses.

The next day it became painfully apparent that Private Beaumont's wounded leg had grown gangrenous. Beaumont, though, did not make it as far as the table before he screamed and tried to run on his savaged leg.

"Hold him," Doctor Dubois said, unrolling the leather and brass buckled tourniquet.

Beaumont fell over, grabbing at Jeremiah until they both tumbled over into the mud and blood and small pile of hacked-off limbs. The skin was a color between blue and gray. Beaumont lay in the mud and howled.

When it was over, Dr. Dubois stood in front of his wash basin trying to clean his hands with what was as much blood as water. "Jeremiah, take a shovel, dig a hole and deposit these unfortunate remains in it, please."

"Yessir." Jeremiah left to find a spade. As ordered, Jeremiah dug the shallow hole, struggling in the mud and the rock-hard earth beneath it. He tenderly placed the remains in the hole and then straightened up to cover them with dirt.

Jeremiah stared at the pail hand that stuck out of the hole. "I can't," he said. If there were more limbs to bury, then he could do it later. He would not have to dig another hole. More importantly, he would not have to see dirt fall upon these pieces of men.

Jeremiah limped back to his small corner of the tent and was asleep before he hit the ground. When the night men ran, he did not hear them.

"Hold his legs, Jeremiah, or he'll be castrated as well as amputated," Doctor Dubois said, the next day at dusk. Calhoun's arm would have to be removed or he would suffer blood poisoning.

Calhoun said nothing. He did not cry or beg or pray. There was something missing from his eyes as he stared at Jeremiah the whole time until he finally, mercifully passed out.

Jeremiah collected the arm in a wooded bucked and took it to the hole. In the settling night, Jeremiah staggered to the edge of the hole and tried to gently drop Calhoun's arm.

The hole was empty.

Jeremiah stumbled backwards almost falling over his own feet. There were any number of perfectly good reasons that the body parts should be missing, but as Jeremiah sat staring into the empty grave, and that's what it was, a grave, not a single one occurred to him.

It was dark by the time Jeremiah reached the surgeon's tent and he was surprised to find it empty. He left the Doctor's quarters and headed for the recovery tent. Jeremiah stood outside the meager glow the lantern in the tent that smelled of sour sweat and infection. He tried several times to swallow, but found that he was unable. The beds in the tent were empty. Empty as Dr. Dubois's tent had been, as empty as the makeshift grave had been.

Jeremiah heard the sound of men running.

Hands shaking, Jeremiah took the lantern and headed off into the woods, following the sounds that, he wondered absently, if anyone else could even hear.

Jeremiah had seen things during the war. He'd seen a man cut clear in half by a cannon shot. He'd seen a man's head explode, the ball shot punching right through his skull. He wondered if the real sin of war wasn't the horrible things that you did, but the horrible things that you witnessed, the horrible things you had to find a way to accept. The man, the one cut in half by the cannonball, his horror was over. Jeremiah, though, carried the horror, as sure as he'd carried the cannonball that cut that Union soldier in half.

Jeremiah startled the men in the woods. They appeared just beyond the light of his lantern. "Identify yourself!"

"Cripple," one of them said.

Jeremiah squinted in the darkness, recognized one of their voices. "Beaumont? What are you doing out of bed?"

Beaumont stepped forward. Jeremiah's eyes flashed to the man's legs. It had returned, though gray and mottled. "Just running around, Jeremiah."

The others stepped into view. The men who had lost legs. The legs, some of them rotting to the bone, had returned.

"What...what happened?"

"A miracle," Calhoun said.

It didn't look like any miracle Jeremiah ever heard of.

"A secret," Lieutenant Danner said.

"The Captain needs to know about this."

"No," Calhoun said, knocking Jeremiah to the ground. The lantern hit the ground, sending the light in furious phantoms against the darkness.

"Wait," the Lieutenant said.

"You held me down while he did this to me." Calhoun struck Jeremiah with the cold meat of his dead hand.

"He's one of us," the Lieutenant said.

"You keep the secret," Beaumont said. "You keep the secret or I'll hold you down..."

Calhoun pulled Jeremiah to his feet. "And this time, I'll have the saw."

In the morning, the remains had returned to their pit and the men to their tents. Whatever was happening, Jeremiah thought, it fled in the face of sunrise. Jeremiah's father, despite being a bastard, had been a God-fearing Christian, and Jeremiah prayed for just an ounce of his father's cast-iron faith.

Dr. Dubois was nowhere to be found, and exhausted from the previous night's discoveries, Jeremiah slept at the floor of the surgeon's tent.

"Jeremiah," a voice called, but it was not Dr. Dubois, instead it was Captain Benning. Embarrassed to be caught sleeping on duty, especially by the Captain himself. "Cap'n Benning, sir," Jeremiah said, eyes still squinting against the gray morning sunlight.

"I need you to see something, son."

The Captain led Jeremiah across the camp to the open grave.

"I had meant to fill this is in," Jeremiah said, wishing he didn't sound so guilty and weak.

"When was the last time you saw, Dr. Dubois?"

"Yesterday...why?"

Benning nodded toward the grave.

Jeremiah's eyes settled into the hole. Just above the lip of the dirt, he could make out the Doctor's shock of white hair."

"Oh, God."

"Do you have any idea who would do this to?"

Jeremiah could feel the weight of men holding him down. He could feel the sharp teeth of the saw biting into his leg, his good leg, they would take his good leg. "No, sir."

The following nights passed in the much the same way. Jeremiah slept in the corner of the tent during the day. There was little food, so no one noticed that he had stopped eating. Without the Doctor, he had little to do and he was left on his own during the day. At night, though, Jeremiah stood guard over the night men.

At first, the men simply ran through the woods, chasing each other. Playing like children. Sometimes they played rounders and made Jeremiah chase the small leather ball when it had gotten knocked into the dark woods. Jeremiah could not help but smile as he watched them as they ran and cavorted on their lost and regained limbs.

The limbs.

Jeremiah squinted in the lantern light as one of the men passed him. Something on the man's dead leg caught his eye. The gray death reached above the scar on his leg.

It was spreading.

Jeremiah felt the air escape his lungs. What did it mean?

"Jeremiah?" Lieutenant Danner startled him.

"Yessir?"

"You look troubled, son."

"I guess so."

"You want to talk about it?"

Jeremiah looked down at the Lieutenant's leg. The dead flesh was above the scar on his leg. "It's spreading, isn't it?"

Lieutenant Danner nodded. He smiled a pained grin. "Thought it would heal, but it aint."

"Are you...dying?"

Danner shrugged. "Stronger than ever, I s'pose...

"Well, that's something."

"But that isn't what you mean, is it?"

Jeremiah shook his head.

"For all I know, I may be dead right now, son."

The Lieutenant looked at Jeremiah and something in the officer's eyes, something dark and absent glared back at the boy. The look of someone ready to kill or someone preparing to die. Jeremiah could not tell the difference or even if there was one.

Jeremiah looked away.

"Bad things, Jeremiah, not just in my leg, but in my head."

"The others?"

"Worse, I think. They've *talked* about the women, the girls at the school."

"What do we do?"

"I need you to do something for me, Jeremiah."

"Anything.

Jeremiah ran. He carried the heavy bottle of lamp oil that the Lieutenant had given him in one hand and the Lucifers in the other. Dusk was settling over the camp.

Jeremiah had to wait until the last minute to light the fire, if he did it too soon, the men would try to put the fire out. After dusk, the men would assume it was one of many of the camp's fires and do nothing.

Lieutenant Danner promised to be the first of the night men to reach the grave, but when Jeremiah got close to the grave, he did not see him.

Jeremiah tripped and went down hard.

The jar of lamp oil shattered on the ground. The acrid smell burned his eyes and nose.

"You worthless little cripple," Calhoun said. The flesh around his face torn and limp. He was as dead as any man could be. "Danner told us your plan...eventually."

"How?"

"Do you think we had to wait until sundown? We couldn't get our legs back 'till then, but I got legs and arms." Calhoun produced the surgeon's saw. It was slick with blood. "Let me tell you my plan, now, cripple. I'm going to go over to that school and see about some horizontal refreshments with some of those fancy girls. Then, I might see how many pieces of them I can cut off before they stop crying." Beaumont and several others were behind him, crowded together near the grave to retrieve their remains. They were beyond dead now, Jeremiah could see. Vacant eyes, hungry, stared at him. "Hold his legs for me, men."

"Please no," Jeremiah tried to get to his feet. The smashed box of Lucifer's were spread out in front of him. He clawed at them. If he could get one lit...

Calhoun stomped on his hand, breaking all of his fingers. Jeremiah could barely gasp as Calhoun brought his foot around into his ribs.

"You got anything to say, cripple?"

Jeremiah tried to fight back the pain, to think of one answer that would save his life. He had none.

"This will only hurt for a minute," Calhoun said, taking Jeremiah's good leg in his hand and settling the blade on it.

This was it.

Jeremiah barked.

The act so took Calhoun by surprise that the he had no response."

"Mad dogs!" Jeremiah's voice was as loud and clear as any Union officer's. He let loose with a wild rallying cry of barks and howls.

The first hornet hit Beaumont in the head. The rifles shots were like rain falling on a metal roof. Calhoun tumbled forward, collapsing under the weight of so many gunshots. Jeremiah could hear the men reloading.

Jeremiah tried to move and found that he could not. He had been hit in the side and he thought his back was broken. He took one of the Lucifers out of the box, lit it and dropped it in the puddle of lamp oil in which they lay.

Jeremiah was dead, truly dead, before the flames took him.

The Gallows

Kaylee couldn't believe McKenzie had run her fat mouth about her trying to kill herself. She ditched her so-called friends on the loser side of the park and stormed off. Burning with angry embarrassment, she dropped herself into one of the little kids' swings. Next to her, one of the empty swings spun in the breeze. She shook her head. "Screw that, I can go faster," she said, kicking her feet out and swinging.

The other swing went higher.

Kaylee kicked her legs harder, yanking backwards on the chain. Her feet went higher.

Next to her, she could see the shadow of the empty swing. It looked like a little girl. In a skirt, with pigtails. Like old photos that she'd seen of herself.

"What...what do you want?"

Silently, the shadow girl increased her speed. Kaylee blinked. In the space between blinks, the shadow girl became a shadow teenage girl hanging by her neck.

"Oh," Kaylee said. She kicked harder, sending her swing even higher.

The sun was starting to go down and the shadow began to spread across the playground toward her like her blood on the bathroom floor.

It's winning, Kaylee thought. *I'm going as high as I can and it's winning.*

Her only chance was to jump, to get as far as she could and hit the ground running. She scrambled to kick as hard as she could, counting down in her head as the shadow girl kept pace with her.

Kaylee jumped, but never landed.

Weighing of the Heart

Mr. Martin lay sprawled on the marble floor of the Ancient Egypt exhibit, his head wrenched backward on his shoulders, eyes blankly staring at the vaulted ceiling of the main hallway.

"I think he's dead," Jeff said, crouching under a glass-topped display table of turquoise and gold jewelry.

"No shit," Dave said, hiding, back pressed against the wall between two life-sized statues of a dog-headed Egyptian deity. Ra? Anubis? What had Mr. M said? Was he really dead? Oh, shit. Oh, shit. Oh, shit. He dug his cell out of his jeans and dialed 911. Nothing. "No signal."

"Downtown, how can you have no bars?"

"How is Mr. M dead? One mystery at a time, okay?"

"No mystery. The mummy got him. You saw it."

"That wasn't a mummy."

"Well, it sure wasn't the Creature from the Black Lagoon."

Dave shook his head frantically. "Guy in a suit, just a guy...dressed up or something."

"I could see through his chest cavity, so, yeah, great disguise."

Alan was crying somewhere, the only geek too lame even to find a place in nerd herd Art Club. His sobbing grew louder and louder.

"Shut up, you pussy," Jeff said, his voice twice as loud as Alan's mewling.

"Who died and made you Lara Croft?"

"You want that mummy to come back?"

Dave bit his lip. The rain pounded the floor to ceiling windows so hard that it was like being inside a car wash.

Alan mumbled something over and over.

"Alan," David said. "Alan, c'mon you have to be quiet, man, please."

"What did he say?"

Dave shrugged. "Alan, c'mon..."

"Mom didn't sign my permission slip."

"Time to go," Jeff said, sliding out from his hiding place.

"Alan," Dave said. "We have to go..."

"I pissed myself," he said. "I fucking pissed myself."

Jeff stood up carefully.

A mummy slammed against the glass behind him. Everyone jumped.

The mummy was suspended inside a glass case. There was nothing below its waist, but it writhed in its display nonetheless. It looked like someone had started making a man out of leather and wire and paper mache, but gave up half-way through. In its gnarled hand, it held a gold staff.

Jeff looked at Dave. "Guy in a suit?"

Dave said nothing.

The mummy's eyeless sockets seemed to focus on them. Its shriveled face twisted into a knot of anger. Jeff read the placard affixed to the glass. "Says he's a priest." The mummy pounded its staff against the inside of the thick glass. *Bang.* Jeff shook his head, knocking his knuckles on the glass. "It won't break." It pounded the glass again, harder and louder. *Bang.*

"Shit," Dave said. "He's calling for help."

Alan stopped crying. "What was that?" A shuffling and a thump in the other room. Moving closer. "Coming back," Alan said. "It's coming back."

Jeff grabbed Dave and dragged him out of the closer of the two doorways that lead out of that section of the exhibit.

"Don't tell my mom," Alan mumbled.

Dave and Jeff left the exhibit as the mummy shambled in. A sign on the wall read: *Please Do Not Touch the Exhibits.* Alan did not scream, but the silence seemed so much worse.

Out in the main hallway that connected the two huge halls of the Ancient Egypt exhibit, Dave and Jeff froze when they saw Mr. M's body. The hallway was lined with smashed and empty display cases that looked like glass coffins. Dave's head felt like it was spinning. He had been talking to Mr. M less than half an hour ago.

"You'll dig this, Dave," Mr. M said conspiratorially, *pulling him aside. See the empty exhibit?"*

"Yeah, what about it?" Mr. M always had *something funny or perverse to share, sometimes perversely funny, so one of his asides was not to be missed. He treated Dave like a person, like a friend, rather than an orphan. The other teachers at Hadley treated him like Oliver Twist, making special, thoughtful comments when they mentioned parents, family or anything they might be deemed insensitive. It made Dave want to puke blood.*

"This exhibit, the whole Egypt exhibit is all from the same archaeological dig, right? Everything was dug up and brought over here, no problem, right? All but that one," he said, pointing to the empty, under-construction exhibit *hall. "Apparently, that mummy was never supposed to leave Egypt. This guy Endsley stole it right under their*

noses back in the 1900's and it took them this long to find it. Huge scandal. Some big pyramid princess."

"Stolen," Dave said. "Like everything in the British Museum."

"Wow," Mr. M said, practically beaming. "Someone listens in my class." They both laughed. "You didn't hear it from me," Mr. M said, dropping his voice. "That art school scholarship is going to go through."

It was Dave's turn to beam. "I don't know how to thank you."

"Just be awesome, okay? Whatever you do, man, be awesome."

"Dead, man, he's gone," Jeff said. The sound of glass smashing in the other room froze them both in their tracks. "Shit."

When they had come up earlier, the staircase had been flanked by two enormous statues of Pharaohs, now the statues completely blocked the stairs. "They moved them" Dave mumbled. They must have weighed a couple of tons apiece.

"We're not going out that way," Jeff said, whirling around.

The mummies were moving closer.

Without a word, Jeff ran, throwing himself through the plastic curtain that sealed off the construction zone. A cartoon mummy held a sign that said *PARDON OUR DUST*.

"Dave?" A girl's voice.

"Vanessa?" A knot of hope twisted in his belly.

A girl poked her head out. Her black hair was pulled into two long pigtails braided with copper wire, purple yarn and ribbon.

"Oh shit, Lainey."

"Why don't you just talk to her?" Dave was hanging out with her in the art room at school a week ago. Lainey

was bending aluminum armature wire for a sculpture that she was planning. The pliers moved gracefully in her hands. The wire bent to her will as easily as everything else in her life did.

"I don't know," Dave said. "She's just so…"

"Yeah," she said. "I know." There was a tone in her voice that suggested that despite being Vanessa's best friend, she might be a little tired of all the attention that she got from guys. "I want to sit next to Jeff in the van."

"Really?"

Lainey stopped bending her wire. She stared at Dave for a minute. "No, not really, you dumbshit, but if I sit next to him, ungh, then you can…"

Dave smiled. Lainey had made it abundantly clear on a number of occasions that she could not stand Jeff. "Be nice…Jeff is my best friend…"

"Yeah, that's great, but Jeff is like half a retard, but I'm willing to take one for the team."

"Dave, Vanessa, they took her and Cayce. The fucking mummies." She pointed towards the under construction wing of the Ancient Egypt exhibit. The Tomb.

"We can't just leave her. We can't." Dave held Lainey's hand and the two of them pushed through the plastic curtain into the tomb. The first chamber of the Tomb exhibit was the largest. The walls were lined with empty glass cases and a large bare dais dominated the middle of the room. The purloined princess, Dave thought.

"Dave, what the fuck is going on?"

Dave shook his head, looking around for something to use as a weapon. For a construction site, the place seemed pretty much baby-proofed.

Something rustled the plastic behind them.

"Jeff?" Lainey's voice was less than a whisper.

"No." Dave looked up, a scaffold covered the wall all the way to the twenty-foot high ceiling. "Climb."

The mummy shuffled into the room, carrying the smaller priest.

Dave froze halfway up the scaffolding, Lainey right beneath him. If the mummies stopped and looked around, they would seem them.

The larger mummy placed the priest down on the floor before the large raised platform and then bowed before it himself, almost grieving.

Oh, shit. He knew what was going on.

After a worshiping at the empty space, the two mummies gathered themselves and moved deeper into the tomb.

"I know what's going on," Dave said.

They crept across the empty chamber to the hallway where the mummies had gone. Dave found a crowbar leaning against the wall, where workers were removing hieroglyphic stone decorations. He picked it up and gave it a swing. Outside, thunder exploded and lightning sparked.

The lights went out.

Lainey grabbed Dave's arm.

"It's okay," he said, not believing his own words.

Somewhere deep in the exhibit ahead of them someone screamed in agony and terror.

"Cayce," Lainey said. "Oh God, that was her."

Hating himself, Dave thanked God that it wasn't Vanessa.

"Aren't you bored?" Vanessa and Dave had shared the middle seat on the school van for the trip. She had been sketching and listening to her iPod for several hours before she turned her attention to him. He had been sitting, doing nothing really and pretending not to sneak glances at her.

Dave shrugged. "Not really. I guess. Yeah."

"No music?"

"Forget my, ya'know," he said, making the gesture of putting on headphones. The truth was that his foster family, his current foster family, was more concerned with cashing the support checks the government sent for him, than with buying expensive gifts. He had learned to live without through a short lifetime of having nothing. It didn't even embarrass him anymore, not really. Vanessa's eyes, something in them, told him that it would not make a bit of difference to her. She had never asked him what it was like not having parents or treated him like Harry Potter because his foster parents sucked donkey balls.

She pulled one ear bud out from beneath her dark hair and offered it to him. "You better like Sarah Mclachlan or this is going to be a long trip." The cord for her headphones were too short and after a minute of adjusting, Dave almost thanked her politely and went back to staring out the window. "Here," she said, leaning against this shoulder. Dave took a deep breath of her and she filled his lungs. He closed his eyes and listened to the music.

Something in the dark moved.

Lainey squeezed his arm so tight, that he almost cried out.

"Jeff?"

The sound stopped.

The darkness was so absolute that it felt like being submerged in oil. Dave dug his cell out. He found it hard to breathe. The air smelled like his foster mother,'s, spice drawer- if a cat had died in it.

Dave flipped his cell open. The LED screen lit up the entire hallway.

Jeff stood in front of them.

"Jesus, man, I called you and..."

"Dave," Lainey said. "His neck..."

Something was wrapped around his neck. A raggedy hand. Holding him from behind. His feet didn't touch the floor.

"Dave," Jeff coughed. The hand squeezed, crushing his larynyx.

Stumbling backwards, Dave dropped his phone, grabbed at it, but only managed to send it skidding across the floor. The light tumbled and flashed off the walls.

Lainey got to the phone first, while Dave was still trying to get to his feet. In the light that   shone from the phone, Dave could see that the mummy was little more than a skeleton wrapped in rags, not the massive creature that had moved the stone statues around. Something struck Dave in the back, knocking him to the floor. Jeff's body. It landed on Lainey and slammed her to the floor.

Dark again. His phone must have broken or landed face down.

Dave scrambled to his feet, got both hands on the crowbar and swung it as hard as he could. It made contact and he heard the sound of dried wood breaking. Bones?

He could feel a bony hand clawing at his leg. He swung the crowbar down.

Lainey shoved Jeff's body out of the way and got the phone. Dave tripped over Jeff, stumbling face-first onto the marble floor.

"You said you knew what was going on?"

"The Egyptian government took the mummy princess back and I think these guys are really pissed," Dave said.

"Why don't they just get a new princess?"

Dave and Lainey stared at each other.

"Oh, no," Lainey said.

"Vanessa."

"She's probably still alive, then."

Dave and Lainey pushed through a large tarp that covered the entrance way to the main chamber. Inside, make-shift torches cast uneven light on the entire chamber.

"Oh my God," Lainey said, covering her mouth and turning away.

Dave dropped the crowbar. It rang on the floor.

They had found Cayce.

"You're a really good artist, Dave," Cayce said. She had won several major art competitions and had already sold several of her paintings.

Dave shrugged, covering up his sketchpad self-consciously. "Just doodling."

"You should talk to Mr. M, show him your work."

"Just embarrassed, I guess."

"Look," she said. "I'll show him your sketches, won't tell him they're yours and see what he says, cool?"

"You're the best."

"Yeah, I know."

She was laying spread eagle on a low platform. A trail of blood ran from her nose to a small dish filled with her brains. Her chest was sliced open and someone had started to remove her insides, separating them into canopic jars that were lined next to her. The room stank of shit and blood and fear.

Tears in his eyes, he swung the crowbar, smashing a glass scarab screwed to the wall.

Shapes crept closer in the darkness behind them, but Lainey couldn't stop looking at what was left of Cayce.

"Where the hell is Vanessa?" Dave frantically searched the hieroglyphic covered walls.

EMPLOYEES ONLY.

He clawed at the hidden door with one hand and then struck it with the crowbar, before finally stabbing it into the door jam. The door creaked open with a puff of construction dust.

Her bandaged body lay just beyond the door in the enormous service elevator. A gold headdress had been placed on her head and she was adorned with gold jewelry.

"Dave," she said, her eyes pleading with him.

"Oh Jesus, Vanessa," he said. "Lainey, we are leaving!" The three of them took the elevator down to the service level. A loading dock led to the street up a steep ramp.

Lainey ran. "I'll get help."

"Can't wait," Dave said, dragging Vanessa out into the street. There was no way of knowing how many more mummies were behind them. Her legs were bandaged together with the ancient wrappings and she could not walk. After a few stumbling steps, Dave picked her up and carried her in his arms. "It's okay," he said. Her gold headdress fell off and he nearly tripped over it. Stumbling down the street away from the museum, he buried his face in her hair, but he could not smell her, only the weird spice aroma and the dead smell of the tomb.

Blocks away, a police siren wailed, moving closer. Help was on its way. Thank God.

"Dave," Vanessa said, coughing.

"Help's coming."

She coughed again, her body convulsing.

Dave stopped, looking behind him to make sure the other mummies weren't coming. There was nothing behind them. He held Vanessa close, as she convulsed again. "What's wrong?"

She stared at him. "Dave?" Blood dripped from her nose.

"Oh my, God, what's wrong?" Gently, he set her down on the wet pavement. Blood began to seep through her bandages. "No. No. No. Fucking no."

She went limp in his arms.

Dave gently undid the bandages covering her chest. Her pale, perfect skin was sliced from throat to groin and then sewn up with rough thread. Shaking, he stood up and lifted her up again in his arms. He took an unsure step back toward the museum. In there she would be alive. He took another step.

A police cruiser skidded to a stop in front of him. The police jumped out and, seeing the blood, drew their weapons. "Put the girl down," one of them shouted.

"I can't," Dave said and ran.

The first bullet caught him in the shoulder, spinning him around. He didn't fall, though, or lose Vanessa's body. Her blood covered his hands, cold compared to his own that ran down his chest.

"No!" Lainey running down the street, her voice frantic.

Dave took another step.

The second bullet went through his back and hit his heart, knocking him forward. He dropped Vanessa's body into the loading dock and it rolled down the concrete slope. He collapsed, dead before he hit the pavement.

"My prince," he heard, hands gently lifting him.

*****

Dave awoke in tight warmth, covered in clean bandages, his face hugged in cool gold. He opened his eyes and saw Vanessa pressed next to him in the dark, together in a stone sarcophagus. He could feel her breasts against his own chest. Her breath was sweet against his lips. His heart was gone, but it beat hard against the inside of his chest. He took a deep breath in missing lungs and she filled him. Her eyes flickered open and, without a trace of fear, focused on him in the dark. He wondered if forever would be long enough.

Cat Got Your Tongue?

"Evil was easier," Samhain said, lifting the enormous stone slab off the mausoleum floor. Beneath it, a crude tunnel led off into the darkness beneath the cemetery. The glinting green eyes of his cat head picked out details that no human being could ever see.

"I would certainly not be the one to remind you that your past evil deeds brought you to your present vocation," said the Jack O' Lantern that he was carrying. It hung from his arm on a black leather strap. When it spoke, which it did far too often for Sam's tastes, flames licked from its triangular eyes and its upturned curve of a mouth.

Sam's whiskers twitched as he dusted his paws, er, hands off. Even after all this time in this body, Sam found it hard to adjust his thinking. "Filthy," he said.

"I was under the impression that proper cats just licked themselves clean," Jack said.

Sam smirked, not sure what Jack was getting at. "I don't feel comfortable having this conversation with a talking gourd."

"So be it." The flickering flames died down. Pouting.

"Besides," Sam said. "Filthy, but not quite as filthy as it should be."

"Something wicked this way *came*?"

Sam nodded. "Think so."

Sam plucked something from the ground.

"A clue?"

"A fun-sized Snickers bar," Sam said

"The missing Trick-or-Treater?"

Sam unwrapped it and popped it into his mouth. He chewed for a second, licked his lips. "Ya'know, Halloween has been my favorite holiday since they made Jack O' Lanterns out of turnips."

"Dark days, indeed."

Sam gestured to the dark cavern that extended beneath the mausoleum and probably the whole cemetery. Sam's ears twitched.

"What is it?"

"I can hear...water."

"Anyway of telling how deep it is?"

"Only one way I can think of," Sam said and dropped Jack down the hole.

"SamHAIN!"

"Don't call me that," Jack said, listening for the splash.

My mistress, my witch, exploded in a gout of green flames and putrid black smoke. The wizard cast his icy gaze around her cave and spotted me, hiding on the top shelf behind a bottle of the blood of virgins. "And you, Samhain, my felonious feline, you and your entire dark-hearted breed of familiar make me ashamed to call myself a cat lover..."

Trying to escape, I leapt.

He caught me in mid-air, seizing me by the scruff of the neck and bringing me eye to eye with him. I hissed and lashed out at him, but to no avail.

"Should you share your witch's fate?" He gathered up a handful of the swirling green flame of my witch's demise and made to cook me like a roast. At the last second, though, an idea seemed to sparkle in his eyes.

I didn't like the looks of it.

Not one bit.

Despite the human race's love of anthropomorphizing animals, turning them in, at least into their imaginations, into little humans (usually children), most animals, as a rule, have no wish to actually become human beings. Except for the entire idiot species of canine, that would give two paws and a tail to walk with the hairless apes.

Cats have no such aspirations I assure you.

"Your witch spread her foul evil about the whole of civilization," the wizard said. "I have no interest in spending my remaining days, no matter how few or many, chasing down and extinguishing all the fires she left burning." He closed his fist and smothered the witch killing flames. "I think the world has a use for you yet." He tossed me to the floor and when I landed, it was on two feet.

"No," I said, but it was done.

Sam dropped himself down through the hole and landed in knee-deep water. "Wet silk," he said, giving his long, black cape a bit of a flap, like shaking the rain off of an umbrella. The cape was another of the wizard's little affectations. The black and orange checked harlequin suit being another... The entire effect was more Saturday-morning cartoon superhero than supernatural knight-errant. "Wet leather," he said, wiping his steel-studded belt and scabbard with his hand.

He lifted Jack out of the water and dumped out the mud. After a moment, Jack sputtered and his flame relit. "I sincerely hope you get an unbearable case of the mange."

Sam shook Jack and his light shone brightly in the tight corridor. In places, thick-hairy roots poked out of the earth and coffins hung down from the ceiling. Skeletal remains in funeral rags greeted them at every turn.

"Charming."

Sam took a few steps, his cape floating like oil on the cemetery runoff. The water behind them bubbled and splashed. Something less than human hissed.

Sam stopped, but did not turn around. "You hear that?"

"I'm afraid so."

Sam grimaced. "Time to clock in." Whirling around, Sam drew his sword and swung high, cutting the creature's head off. One of its heads, at least.

The beast that stood before them could barely be contained in the tunnel. Long and lean, it sported a surplus of horns, claws and fangs, so many, in fact, that it was hard to tell which of the three protrusions were which.

The remaining heads hissed angrily.

Sam retreated a few steps keeping his eyes on the creature. He spun his sword in his hand, faster and faster, like the propeller of a small plane, building momentum for the moment when...

The creature lunged at him and he relieved it of its other two heads.

"Two-for-one without a coupon," Jack said, as the body slunk down into the water. He sheathed his sword and held up Jack to retrieve the evil soul.

Nothing happened.

Sam smacked the Jack O'Lantern like a TV remote that wasn't working.

Still nothing.

"Odd," Jack said. "And...ouch!"

"Every monster has a dark soul," Sam said. "Something's wrong."

"We should tread lightly, we are in uncharted territory."

Sam opened his mouth to offer some feline wit, but only nodded his head. He continued down the tunnel, stepping carefully on the uneven floor. He had no intention of stepping off a ledge and winding up over his head in filthy muck.

"Why do you think this thing, whatever it is, stole this child?"

"Honestly?"

"Of course."

"Monsters snatch adults for a reason. Revenge, maybe. Treasure. A mate."

"Children, then?"

"Kids? Kids are for eating. Pure and simple."

"That's possibly the most heinous thing I've ever heard you say."

"You asked."

The two of them slipped into silence as they slipped through the curves of the tunnel. Sam noticed right away that the tunnel had been dug, not built and that was, in his expertly evil opinion, a bad sign. A tunnel ten-foot round was dug by a sizable beast. Suddenly, his weapon seemed rather short.   Sam stopped and drew his sword.

"What?"

"Something...just...touched...my...foot," Sam said.

It seized his ankle and jerked him off his feet.

"Wet silk," he said. "Wet silk, wet leather...wet furr!"

The tentacle dunked him into the water head first. Jack went flying, a trail of flame following the arc of his descent.

Sam sprung from the water, gasped a lungful of air and was pulled under again.

Jack landed on the lid of a fallen coffin. "Sam! Sam!"

Sam broke the surface of the water again, hacking downward at the tentacle beneath him.

"Did you get it?"

"Does it look like I got it?" Sam was pulled under again, but sprung back up. "I think there's just the one and..."

Several writhing tentacles exploded from the water.

Sam took his sword in both hands, ready to swing as hard as he could. "Too many of them..."

"Get down," Jack said, fire leaping from his eyes and mouth.

Sam could feel the heat on his fur. He knew what that meant. He ducked down into the muck.

From beneath the water, Sam could hear Jack scream something and saw a fireball fill the tunnel. The tentacles burst into flame, lashing at each other and writhing in agony. When the flames faded, around the same time Sam ran out of air, he sprung up out of the water and made short work of the smoking remains with his sword. He picked up Jack and held him aloft to gather the monster's soul, but he was not surprised that nothing happened.

"Again?"

"I think I know what's going on," Sam said, as they followed the tunnel to where it opened up to a large, terrible space. The lair.

A little girl dressed in a black dress stood at the opening of another tunnel that branched off the large chamber. Her eyes lit up when she saw that someone had come for her, but her shoulders slumped when she saw that Sam was just another monster come to terrorize her.

"Come on, kid," Sam said. "We have to get out of here."

"That door," Jack said.

"Yeah, I see it."

"It has...teeth."

"Doors don't have teeth," Sam said.

The door roared, spitting slime and filth at them. The little girl bent like a palm tree in a hurricane.

"Look out!" The girl had attempted a scream, but hoarse from crying, she managed only a strangled cough.

Sam whirled around. The monsters had returned. The three-headed creature, all horns, fangs and claws was back. The swirling mass of tentacles had returned as well.

"Didn't we kill them already?" Jack was sparking in anger. He would not be able to repeat his supernova trick again for days, maybe weeks.

Sam didn't think they had that long. This was becoming the worst rescue in the history of rescues. "Little girl, you have to come to me."

Terrified, she stood still.

The enormous mouth stood so close behind her, that Sam was afraid that even if she did move, it might just snap shut on her. Each fang was taller than the girl herself.

The monsters were closing in behind them. It looked like the big one was going to let his stooges do the dirty work. That didn't make much sense, though, Sam thought. He had already beaten them once. The big mouth was taking a risk not finishing him off itself. Unless...

"I think it's just a mouth," Sam said.

"Isn't that enough?" Jack panicked.

Sam darted left and then hurried back right, trying to make out the shape of the monster that provided a home for that enormous mouth, but he could see nothing. "Just a mouth," he said. "That means..." Sam plunged his hand down in the water and after a moment pulled up a gray-white tube the thickness of a fire hose. "This is its tongue!"

The monsters stopped. They were all connected to the bizarre umbilicus, the miles of pseudopod tongue.

Sam raised his sword high over his head and brought it down on the tongue in a flash.

The giant mouth howled, making the tunnel shake. Chunks of earth and coffins fell splashing in the water. The monsters fell limp. The entire tunnel began to collapse.

"One last thing," Sam shouted and ran into the creature's open mouth. After a moment, the howling stopped and Sam reappeared, blood dripping from his sword. He lifted Jack up and a blue flame leapt from the creature's mouth and into the waiting pumpkin. That's how it was done.

A massive chunk of the tunnel fell into the water with a splash.

"All done, gotta go," Sam said, grabbing the girl around the waist. He didn't stop running until they were back outside the mausoleum. They stood dripping for a long time.

"Is that...a mask?" The little girl was shaking even as she mustered the courage to speak.

Sam shook his head. "I'm afraid not."

The girl bit her lip. "Do you...miss being a kitty?"

Sam sighed. "Very much."

She gestured to him and when he bent to her, she rubbed behind his ear. After a moment, he purred. "Good kitty."

"Not yet, but I'm trying," Sam said. He dusted her pointy witch hat off and set it on her head. "Ya'know, I used to know a real witch."

"Was she nice?"

Sam grinned. "Not even a little."

The little girl laughed. "Well, you do have a very nice Jack O'Lantern."

"Thank you," Jack said.

"He talks!"

"Endlessly," Sam said, picking her trick-or-treat bag up from the graveyard grass. Brown slime splashed from it.

"Ick. My candy is all ruined."

"Looks like," Sam said. "Well, maybe if there is a little time left, we could hit a few houses before I take you back to your mom and dad."

"Really?"

"Sure." The little witch took Sam's paw, er, hand and he led her out of the cemetery toward bright colored lights and happy laughter.

inaccessible

Scott sat in his wheelchair staring at the zombies swarming around the street in front of his parent's modest, two-story suburban home. It was the only parade he'd gotten since he got home from Iraq. He cursed. Twice as many as there were yesterday. He was reasonably sure that they did not know he was here, but he didn't know why they chose his street for their little block party. He ran his fingers through his close-cropped black hair and cursed again. He figured it was too much to ask that the apocalypse would come with wheel chair ramps.

He glanced out the window again. His modified truck sat at the curb. He estimated that it was about a hundred yards away. He rolled back from the window and looked at his trophy shelf. Football. Baseball. Basketball. In high school, he could run a hundred yards in 9.2 seconds. In Iraq, even in full battle rattle, he was sure he'd run faster than that. He swept all the trophies off the shelf with one arm. The room had been his bedroom in high school and now he wished that he had not come in here. It had the best view of the street, though.

He rolled back to the window. The zombies were still there.

His roommates, James and Dave, had been gone for a week and he doubted that they were coming back. Either they made it to safety and couldn't face returning for him or, more likely, they had not made it. Over the past week, he'd spent quite a bit of time wondering about them. Sometimes, when he was feeling the most sorry for himself, he hoped they didn't make it, but Dave and James were good guys, they'd been there for him when he got out of the service and, mostly, he hoped they'd succeeded.

It had actually been his own plan, even the part about leaving him behind. Rooftop to rooftop through the suburbs where the houses were no more than ten feet apart. A good plan that immediately excluded him. The zombies were actually smarter than they looked and if they could manage to get up the stairs, they'd be screwed. They used Scott's Dad's ladder to bridge the gaps.

Scott stayed behind under the pretense of providing cover fire, but the others were gone so fast that the zombies didn't even notice they had left. He sat with the Glock on his lap and watched them go.

That was a week ago.

Scott's stomach growled. He rolled back to his parent's room in the back of the house. They had been using this room as their living quarters since all of this had gone down. It was safer to stay off the ground floor, too many windows, and Scott didn't have the option since the electricity was off and his wheel chair lift was dead. He opened the last can of green beans and sat quietly eating them. For all the joking they did about the MREs back in the sandbox, he would have loved to have a nice stack of them right now.

Scott finished the green beans, drank the water from the can and then went into the bathroom and drank three more cans of water out of the bathtub, ignoring the slightly soapy taste. When he was finished, he went back to the window and continued watching the zombies.

Something had their attention and as Scott watched them, he soon figured out what it was. A gray squirrel. Twenty or thirty zombies staggering hungrily after one lone squirrel. A smile turned up the corner of Scott's lip. Absently, Scott wondered what squirrel tasted like, not that he had any better a chance to catch one as they did, but it was a nice distraction. "Motherfucker," Scott said. That was exactly what he needed. A distraction.

Scott spent the rest of the afternoon gathering things he would need and quietly dropping them down the stairs. Towels. Sheets. Several of his father's belts. His Junior high football helmet. A battery-operated stereo.

When he was finished, he carefully climbed out of his wheelchair to the floor. He sat at the top of the stairs, useless legs pointing down and lowered himself step by step to the ground floor. With each step he moved his folded wheelchair with him. Once he got down to the bottom of the steps, he unfolded his chair and eased himself in. He gather up the things he'd thrown down, stacking them on his lap, and went into the kitchen. From the junk drawer, he took a roll of gray duct tape.

Scott occasionally glanced out the windows as night settled on the neighborhood. He didn't know if zombies slept, but he doubted it. Whatever he did tonight, he would have to do it in the dark. Scott's mechanical wheelchair, which he nicknamed *Frankenstein* after the ugly Marine Corps monster trucks in Iraq, sat unused in the corner between the bookcase and his mother's piano. He glared at it like it was a living thing. It made him feel like Stephen Hawking just to have it. He checked the battery and found that it was still charged. How much charge it had would remain to be seen. He figured out a way to maneuver it back over to the couch.

He sat for a minute to catch his breath. He felt hunger stir in his insides. A soldier does not starve to death hiding in his parent's house, he thought. He had faced challenges in his life head on and this would be no different.

He had made his decision as soon as he'd seen those zombies chasing that squirrel. He would live or die, but it would happen on his own terms.

He was going to run for it.

Scott duct taped his basic training boots to the footrests. Then, he stuffed a pair of pants and a long sleeve shirt with towels and sheets, making a rudimentary scarecrow, which he then taped into the chair. The football helmet went on top. He put the radio on the thing's lap and taped it down. The CD inside was *Guns N' Roses*. "Welcome to the Jungle," he said to himself. When arts and crafts was over, he settled down on the couch, in complete darkness and fell asleep.

Hunger woke Scott up like a dog wanting to be let out to pee. He scratched the stubble on his face and yawned. This was the big day.

Scott's scarecrow looked terrible. It slouched in the wheelchair like a drunk and the football helmet head hung to one side. He ripped off a few more strips of tape and tried to fix it up a little bit. He was going to MacGyver his way out of this or die trying.

The zombies were up already. He imagined one of them making coffee somewhere. He pictured them clocking in. Standing in line like extras in a horror movie. Except now life was a horror movie. He laughed. He didn't remember the last time he had actually laughed. It was either a good sign or a horrible one. At this point, Scott didn't give a shit. He had more important things to do.

The Glock 9mm held fifteen rounds and one in the chamber. Scott had loaded it himself. He would have preferred something that did not feel like a toy, but you play the hand that you're dealt. If he had learned anything in combat it was that wishing did not work. Too much of life was wasted wishing for things to be better instead of trying to make them better. No more wishing. There were seven shotgun shells in a box in his father's closet, he loaded his hunting rifle and set it across his lap. That would be fine close-up, but from a distance it would be hard to guarantee a head shot. "No guarantees then," Scott said. "Check. No guarantees. No wishing."

He used his father's belts to strap himself in his chair. It would not serve to fall out of the chair if things got hinky. He steered both chairs to the front door and peeked out from behind the curtains.

The zombies hobbled by. For some reason they seemed to follow the streets and sidewalks. Maybe some kind of memory thing, Scott thought.

"This is suicide," Scott said. His voice was reassuring even if the sentiment was not. He smiled and pushed the mechanical chair out onto the front porch, aiming it down the wheelchair ramp the government had installed for him. "Go long," he whispered into the ear hole of the football helmet. He pushed the steering stick forward and quickly taped it down. The chair leapt forward, giving him only a second to hit play on the stereo. The opening chords of *Welcome to the Jungle* rang out.

Scott ducked back into the house and watched.

The scarecrow got to the bottom of the ramp and shot straight across the grass. By the time it reached the street, the music was blasting.

The zombies turned to watch it go.

Scott laughed.

The zombies just stood there for a minute.

"C'mon."

The zombies chased after the scarecrow.

"Time to go," Scott said and rolled out onto the porch and down the wheel chair ramp. He built up speed on the down slope and grabbed his left wheel to make a turn on one wheel. He thought he would roll and the whole thing would be over, but he did not care.

He couldn't fight his smile.

He was halfway across the grass when the first zombie appeared. Scott didn't try to slow down, he just aimed the pistol and fired off a round into the thing's face. The zombie went down hard, skull smashing against the asphalt.

Trying to steer the wheelchair with one hand while holding the pistol with the other and keeping the shotgun on his lap, was too much. He hit the curb and flipped the chair.

The zombies stopped when they heard the shot.

Scott could see the brain-damaged indecision on their faces.

They turned and moved toward Scott, hurrying, moving faster and faster down the street.

"Shit," Scott said, pushing himself up with one arm and squeezing off a shot. The round hit a dead woman in the gut, but she didn't even flinch.

Scott crawled toward the truck, dragging the shotgun behind him.

The zombies were close.

He didn't have time to get into the truck. Instead, he crawled underneath it.

The first zombie to stick his head under the back of the truck got a round in the face.

After that, though, they swarmed underneath, crawling towards him, hissing though mouths of bloody, broken teeth. Scott pointed the shotgun at them, not even aiming and pulled the trigger.

The explosion was deafening under the truck.

Beyond the pile of corpses at the back of his truck, Scott could more zombies coming. It must have been the ones that had taken the bait and chased the scarecrow.

Scott rolled out from under the truck on the passenger side. The driver's side had an elaborate seat that lowered down and it took too long. Scott sat himself up using the shotgun as a crutch and the reached up to the door handle.

It was too high.

"Fuckfuckfuck!"

A fat teenager in a *System of a Down* t-shirt appeared at the front of his truck. His guts dangled in front of him.

He rushed towards him, even as Scott could hear the footfalls of the other zombies coming.

Scott shot the boy in the face. The body collapsed in front of him.

The zombies were coming, more now. It looked like *all* of them.

"Fuck."

Scott grabbed the teenager by one flabby arm and dragged him toward him. When he was close enough, he eased himself up on the dead kid's back. "Thanks, man," Scott said.

He reached up and unlocked the passenger door, swung it open and pulled himself in.

A zombie grabbed his leg.

Scott shot it in the face, but it didn't die. It reared back to bite.

He squeezed off another shot and its head exploded. Scott threw himself back toward the driver's seat, pulling the door behind him.

All over the zombies were pounding on the truck.

Scott turned the key and the engine roared to life.

The truck rocked. They were trying to flip it.

Scott stomped the gas pedal and the truck shot forward. In the rear-view mirror, he could see the zombies chasing him. They didn't even stop when he pulled ahead. They didn't stop even when he could barely see them in the rear view mirror.

"That's the spirit," he said. "Never give up."

Where the Light Don't Reach

Just before midnight, Emrey showed up at the town jail to take his turn sitting with the prisoner the night before his hanging. Soon as he got there, though, he knew something was wrong.

Sitting behind the old oak desk, Sheriff Teel was perfectly still and, for just a second, Emrey thought he might be asleep. His eyes adjusted to the light inside the jail and he realized that Teel's eyes were open, staring straight ahead.

"Sheriff?"

No answer.

"Sheriff Teel?"

"Emrey," he said as if the word had no meaning for him. He shook his head and rubbed his eyes with his fists. "Emrey, right on time." Sheriff Teel seemed befuddled as he stood up. "Thanks for coming."

"Glad to help," Emrey said, strapping his gun on. "Prisoner been quiet?"

Teel didn't answer right away and it gave Emrey the impression that the Sheriff was considering his answer carefully. Teel was a kind man and one of the calmest personalities that Emrey had ever encountered. He had not really ever known his own father, but when he thought of him, often he pictured Sheriff Teel. He pulled his long coat on and adjusted his hat. "Don't want you talking to the prisoner, Emrey. You ain't got nothing to say to one another. Understand?"

"Yessir."

The Sheriff passed Emrey on the way to the door. "I'll come by with Father Gilbert in the morning and we'll get this done with."

Emrey nodded his head.

Sheriff Teel paused in the doorway. Framed by the darkness outside, he seemed to fade like some kind of ghost. "If Drevanche tries to escape...you shoot him." He stared at the floor. "'Till there ain't no more bullets left. Understand?"

Emrey stared at the Sheriff, unable to think of anything to say back. This seemed enough for him and he turned and left without another word.

Emrey sat through the night as his cheap pocket watch ticked off the hours. He went and stood by the door when the merry crowd of drunks, gamblers and carousers left the saloons to go home. No big winners kicking up their heels or big losers damning their luck. Mason's latenighters drifted past the jail like a peaceful creek, though they gave the jail a wider berth than usual. He couldn't blame them, though. The prisoner was like every ghost story their momma's ever told them, 'cept in the flesh and blood.

Folks in town said that the prisoner was a dyed-in-the-wool madman, others said he wasn't a man at all, but a demon straight from the devil's own hell, but they all agreed on two things. First, that the man should be put to death for his crimes. Second, that he should be buried far from here. Even dead, especially dead, he frightened them.

Emrey went back inside and sat down. He ran his hands over the smooth oak desktop. He had gotten so much pleasure out of building that thing last summer. If he thought he could make a living at it, he would hang up his badge and be a carpenter. He knew that the father of his girl, Annabelle, would never give his blessing for her to marry no lawman. Just no way to do it, he thought. Something caught his eye.

A bird's skull, like a buzzard or a hawk's, sat on the table. It was strung on a rough piece of twine with a few shiny stones and feathers and a bead of green glass.

Emrey leaned back in the chair. Had it been there before? If it had, then he hadn't noticed it. Must belong to the prisoner. Emrey yawned into his fist, standing up from the chair. The thing gave him the frighteners. He was tired and spooked and he hadn't noticed it before, that was all. He was falling asleep anyway, so it was worth taking a minute to stretch his legs. He stood in front of the wall of wanted posters, yellow with age and faded. He wondered how many of those bad hombres had died an ugly death since their faces had been hanging on that wall.

He inspected each face until he came to the new poster. *Drevanche.* What kind of name was that anyway? That was when he heard a voice call his name.

He stared at the heavy oak door that led back to the jail's cells.

"Curiosity killed the cat," Emrey said, and like a good cat he went back to see what the hell was going on.

The back of the jail was divided into two cells. They had split up the one large cell after two out-of-town drunks beat each other near to death after a friendly dispute turned less then friendly. One was empty, the other not.

The prisoner sat in the back of the left cell, crouched on the bed like an enormous black bird. He was a big negro fella and he wore a suit jacket and pants, but no shirt or shoes. During the day, he looked like a rich man who had fled his own wedding. At night, though, Emrey noticed that he looked like a dead man fled his grave. His top hat sat neatly on the bed next to him.

"You say something, Drev-anch?"

"Not I," the man said. He added,"Dray-vonch," all fancy and French and a little reverent like he was speaking the name of the Lord in Sunday service.

"Pardon," Emrey said, extending a politeness that he did not mean to.

Drevanche bowed his head.

"Anyways, you hear something?"

Drevanche smiled a wide, white smile. "Only ghosts."

It was Emrey's turn to smile. "Probably not a lot of ghosts back here."

"I bring my own," the prisoner said.

"Imagine you do," Emrey said. "Sheriff said you killed a few men in your time."

"Indeed I did. And women and children..."

Emrey blinked, the smile fading from his face. "How many you figure?"

Drevanche shook his head clicking his tongue. "Nowhere near enough, I suppose, but that isn't your question is it?"

"What do you mean?"

"You want to know what it's like. To kill a man."

"Sheriff Teel killed a few...in the line of duty, I mean."

"Of course, but he'll tell you it had to be done and how he got sick after and cried and couldn't look at his children..."

"Well, how do you know I haven't killed nobody?"

Drevanche smiled. "Murder leaves a mark on a man." He showed his palm and in the center of the dark flesh was a scar that looked like a skull. He passed his other hand over it like a fast-talking cardplayer and it seemed to vanish. Emrey couldn't look away and it made him feel like a rube. "You want to know what it *really* feels like. You could, you know."

"Could what?"

"Don't insult my intelligence, boy. Just because I don't wear shoes, don't mean I ain't been around. You could reach out and snatch the life right out some poor soul before he even saw you reach for your gun." His voice was dark and rich with a hint of something deadly underneath, like sweet molasses with broken glass in it.

Emrey glanced at the empty food plate. "Food okay?"

"As last meals go, one of the finest I ever had," Drevanche said. "Somebody's Momma went through all that trouble for little ol' me. Not your Momma, though."

"My mother's dead."

"Emrey," the voice came again. A woman's voice. He tried not to recognize it, but failed.

Drevanche leaned against the bars, almost face to face with Emrey. He hadn't seen the man move, but there he was, smelling of strange spices and the rich earth of the grave. "You sure 'bout that, now?"

Out of the corner of his eye, he saw that the other cell, the empty one, was no longer empty. Two figures had filled it. One was close up and the other seemed to drift back where the light didn't reach.

Emrey ran.

He puked outside next to the Jail. He would have gone around back, as he didn't want anyone seeing him, but the dark back there was so absolute that he could not bear to face it. A knot of ice-cold terror formed in his belly that did not go away no matter how much he puked. He wiped his mouth on his shirt sleeve, his good shirt, and went back inside.

He was hearing things or seeing things or both. That voodoo fella had said things, got him thinking, that was all. Gave him the spooks and here he was a grown man afraid of ghosts in the town jail.

Emrey drew his pistol and went back into the cells.

His mother stood just inside the previously empty cell.

"Momma?"

Behind her, in the dark, a smaller form lurked.

Emrey tried to keep his attention on his mother. She was whole and alive, not like the last time he had seen her. Not at all like the last time he had seen her.

Emrey's mother reached out and touched his belly. Her fingers were icy cold.

Emrey rubbed the cold spot in his belly and was surprised when it began to spread up to his chest and down to his legs.

Emrey's head spun and he fell down into the cold.

Emrey lay on his belly on the frozen ground with his mother, watching her take careful aim with his father's rifle. They only had one shot. To reload would take too long, the rabbit would be gone. They hadn't eaten in a good week and the rabbit looked so good that he wasn't even sure he would cook it first. His father hadn't been gone a year yet and ten-year-old Emrey was already starting to forget what the man looked like. One thing he didn't forget, though, was the food that his father brought home. The deer, and possums and sometimes rabbits.

"Now you remember," Emrey's mother said, whispering as she drew a bead on the rabbit. "Gun is just another tool. Just because some bastard used one on your Poppa, God rest his soul, don't mean you gotta be afraid of one. You pound a nail with a hammer and you kill rabbits

with a gun. They don't feel it, just like your Poppa didn't feel it, you understand that, right?

Emrey grunted.

"We call that humane."

"Humane."

"That's right." The rifle barked. "Damn it to hell," *his mother said.*

Emrey's shoulders drooped. The cold had made him numb, all but his hunger. They had a handful of bitter roots they could eat, but it would only go so far with the three of them.

"You cold, Emrey?"

"No'Maam."

"Now don't lie to me boy, that's not how I raised you. You go inside and warm up by the fire. I'll wait for that damn rabbit to come around again."

"Yes'Maam."

Halfway back to the house, his mother called to him again. "Send your sister out to help me."

Emrey stopped. His sister, Susan, had been born crippled, in her body and her head, and she could manage next to nothing. She certainly couldn't help catch no skittish rabbit. "I can stay out," he said.

"When did I have to start telling you everything twice?"

Without another word, he turned and headed back to the house. He bundled Susan up and sent her out. Huddled in front of the meager fire, Emrey heard a shot. He wondered if his mother had managed to get the rabbit. Before too much longer, though, he heard another shot. The two women had been out for a long time and when they hadn't reappeared, even just to warm up, Emrey went outside to see.

He found the two of them dead in the snow.

Shaking, Emrey could only stare at the bodies. Had the bad men come back? The ones who killed his father? No. It was clear even to a ten-year-old what had happened.

Emrey took the rifle, reloaded it as best he could remember how, sat on the ground and put the rifle in his mouth. It tasted of fire and gunpowder. He reached for the trigger, but couldn't get it.

The rabbit reappeared.

A fist of absolute rage seized Emrey and, without as much as aiming, he shot that rabbit dead. He wanted to reload the rifle and join his mother and sister, but he couldn't. The rabbit lay on the cold ground and he couldn't. He took it inside and cooked and ate it. It sustained him for days, even when he tried to crack the frozen earth to bury his sister and mother. A day after that, a deer wandered close to the house and without really even trying Emrey, shot it. He took no joy in it, but he ate the meat and survived the winter.

Emrey felt small, loving hands gently placing a rope around his throat. "This isn't happening," he said, trying to keep his dinner down.

"It's alright," Emrey's mother said.

Emrey felt dizzy. Rocking forward, he realized dreamily that he was standing on the edge of one of the benches.

"Momma," Emrey said, feeling darkness behind his eyes.

"Emrey," a little sweet voice said. Susan. His sister.

"Susan, help me."

She drifted forward from the darkness, her face masked beneath her bonnet. "Emrey...," she said. Her face was a bloody hole in her head, teeth hanging, dangling from the broken remains of her skull. "You eat good, Emrey?"

Emrey toppled back off the bench and felt the noose tighten as he fell.

Pistol still in his right, Emrey clawed at his neck with his left. He dangled on the end of the rope, twisting in the wind.

The door that led to the jail was still open and Emrey could see an eerie green light washing through the doorway.

The necklace. Drevanche's necklace.

The green bead glowed like a coal from a fire.

Drevanche was doing this somehow.

Darkness creeping around his vision, Emrey raised his pistol and fired at the green bead.

He never saw where the bullet hit.

A man named Sutter, who ran the livery stable, was the only one who heard the shot and came running with both of his sons and their shotguns. He cut Emrey down, but it was too late. He sent one son for Doctor Kincaid and the other for Sheriff Teel.

"Why, Emrey?" Sheriff Teel stood in the jail after Callahan had taken Emrey's body. Father Gilbert had said words over the boy's mortal remains.

"Needed a carpenter," Drevanche said. "Jesus was a carpenter, wasn't he, Father? Went by way of the wood and nails. Rose from the dead. A *zombie*. *Drink my blood and live forever!* Like the *vampyre*. Bless his name!"

Father Gilbert returned his small Bible to his coat pocket. "Where you're going, son, there will be fire."

"Where I'm going," Drevanche said. "I will be King!"

Sheriff Teel shook his head. Something caught his eye and he stepped out into the front room of the jailhouse. "Last thing Emrey ever did in this life was put a bullet in this desk, not the width of my finger from your little trinket here."

Drevanche's smile faded. "That is mine."

Sheriff Teel, despite the tears in his eyes, managed a smile. "Really? Why you think Emrey would do a fool thing like that? Me? I'd have shot you. Not old Emrey. He knew how things worked. How people worked. He did it for a reason, didn't he?"

Drevanche's face was pinched. "I am a condemned man and I demand that my possessions be buried with me."

"You demand. *Demand?*" Sheriff Teel drew his pistol and, holding it by the barrel brought the butt down on the necklace, smashing the skull and the stones, and the green glass bead.

Drevanche screamed like a man being branded.

He hammered it until there was little left but debris. "Take him out to the oak tree," Sheriff Teel said, shaking his head.

Several men took Drevanche out of the jail. Father Gilbert followed. They went without a sound.

Sheriff Teel sat in the chair facing the open door to the cells. Although the cells were empty, he got up after a moment and shut both, locking them. He didn't know, though, if that was enough to keep the ghosts in or not

Nothing But Dark

Even in the dark, Paul could still see the old blood stain on the sleeve of his skeleton costume. Bobby died a year ago tonight, an eleven-year-old struck by a car on Halloween night, but the grief still sat on Paul's chest like a cinder block. He had held his friend's hand until there had been nothing left in his eyes. Now, he clenched Bobby's pocket knife in his hand as he moved through the dark woods.

"It's not the devil," Bronwyn said. She looked perfect in her fairy princess costume, her wings sparkled. She was Bobby's older sister and this had been her idea.

"How did you even find out about this thing?" Alex followed close. He was Jason from Friday the 13th, hockey mask flipped up like a welder between welds. Bronwyn collected boys like a bright light collected moths. Paul was not immune.

"I had a dream," Bronwyn said.

It found *her*, Paul thought, wondering if the bright light that he had compared her to wasn't a bug zapper. Or an oncoming train.

Ahead of them, gray-green light bled from a pile of massive pumpkins and twisted vines.

"Is this what's supposed to happen?"

Bronwyn said nothing.

Just as scared as us, Paul thought. "Bron?"

The heap moved, lifting with the weight of an elephant getting to its feet. Arms unfolded from the central mass, causing Paul to take a shaky step back. A head rose into view, a crude Jack O'Lantern. No candle flickered inside this pumpkin, though. Black eyes watched the kids as they shook with fear.

"You have nothing to fear from me," the thing said. "I am the eternal spirit of All Hallow's Eve. We've come to an agreement, Bronwyn?"

She nodded. "Yes."

"Bobby wants to come home, dear," the thing said, sweeping a pile of dry leaves and branches away. Beneath it lay a dark mass. Bobby's body.

"Oh shit," Alex said.

"Do not be afraid, Alexander," the thing smiled, a dark curve. "Each of you have agreed, then?"

Everyone nodded. Somehow it seemed easier to sell your soul, or at least part of it, if you didn't actually have to say it out loud. That was the plan, then, each of us contribute part of our soul to bring Bobby back.

The massive creature produced a burlap sack. "Each of you place some candy, an offering, if you will, into my sack."

Paul could not stop staring at Bobby's body.

Bronwyn dropped a handful of candy into the creature's bag.

Alex glanced at Bronwyn. She nodded once. "Okay," he said, and dropped in a fistful of candy.

Paul shook his head. "I don't think this is a good idea," he said, hands shaking.

"There's no reason to be afraid...," the thing whispered.

Something tickled Paul's fingers. He glanced down and saw that the dried blood on his costume had soaked through the fabric and was now dripping down his arm. It traced the lines of his hand, drawing a handprint across his palm where he had held Bobby's hand as he died.

Tears welled up in Paul's eyes as he could feel Bobby's hand in his own. Something tugged on his hand, trying to lead him away. Paul's eyes flicked to the dark heap. "That...that isn't Bobby."

"Of course it is," Bronwyn said. "The spirit just needs a little to bring Bobby back. Please, Paulie. Please."

There had been a time when he would have done anything for her. Even this. "No. I can't." Paul turned away, back toward the woods.

The spirit-thing took a giant fistful of candy from his sack and devoured it in one bite.

Alex collapsed, dead before he hit the ground.

The spirit-thing licked its fingers. "Sweets for the sweet," it said.

"What the hell?" Paul froze.

The spirit-thing smiled an empty grin. "Couldn't help myself."

"Get away from that thing, Bron," Paul said.

The thing loomed over Bronwyn. "Give me the candy or I'll tear her to bloody shreds."

"Please don't let it hurt me, Paulie, please. "

Paul took a handful of candy and stepped to the enormous sack. "Okay...just don't hurt her." Something squeezed his hand frantically.

Paul stopped, handful of candy dangling over the spirit-thing's sack. He stared at Bronwyn, her eyes slick with tears, her body shaking. "You're...you're not that good of an actress, Bron." He dropped the candy back into his own bag.

She stopped crying and stood up straight. She nodded, almost smiling. "Give him the candy, Paulie."

"It's going to kill us," Paul said.

"Not...us," Bronwyn said, turning her back on him. "Alex...you...your parents if you don't give him your candy."

"Why?"

"Bobby was...my brother. How can you even ask me that?" She couldn't seem to make eye contact with him. "It's you or your parents, Paul. You choose."

Paul dug his hand into his bag, took a handful of candy and dropped it into the spirit-thing's bag.

"I'm sorry, Paul..."

"Go to hell, okay, Bron?"

She nodded. "Probably." She turned to the thing that wasn't Bobby. Did she even care? It began to move beneath the leaves.

The thing shoveled Paul's candy into its gaping mouth. "Very nice, very..."

It choked.

Bronwyn's face went slack.

Paul looked away as the creature collapsed, clawing at its throat as black blood spurted from its neck.

Screaming, Bronwyn collapsed on the head of Bobby's remains, which had gone suddenly still. "What did you do? Paul? Paul, what did you do?"

"It wasn't him, Bron, it wasn't..." Paul tore the bloody pocket knife from the dead thing's throat. He reached out to Bron, but, even as she wailed over the empty pile of leaves, he could see there was nothing left of her.

A Hungry Winter

It was too cold for the living, Jimmy Connolly thought, but apparently, not too cold for the dead. He'd started hearing phantoms before the snow had even begun, calling his name in breathless whispers that he did his best to ignore.

They were hungry and they were searching.

He was headed for the shelter for the night when he saw the first of the phantoms. It flickered in and out of his sight, drifting down the street following a group of street people, like a fragment of rag caught in the wind. It would take one of them that night, he was sure of it. It would come with icicle fangs and frozen claws and sweep them away into the blizzard. They would feed and move on. It would be safer in a day or so.

He couldn't go that way, then. The phantoms chose the weaker ones and he was among the weakest.

The wind snuck up and slashed him to the core. He wore three coats and even they offered little protection. With his parka and hood, he looked every bit of the raggedy reaper.

A phantom slid out from beneath a snow covered bench. It slithered toward him across the snow.

Watching over his shoulder, he ran into a girl on the street. "I'm so sorry," Jimmy said, helping her to her feet. The girl had green hair and kind eyes. She was maybe half his age. She was carrying a pile of pink flyers. Jimmy picked them up from the gray slush on the sidewalk and did his best to wipe them off. "It's okay, really," she said. "Hey, do you have a place to stay tonight? It's going to get cold." She handed him a flyer.

"Thank you," Jimmy said.

"We'll be open at the shelter all night," she said.

Jimmy hurried away down the street.

Jimmy found the weird crate in an alley on 183rd street and crawled in, pulling the flap closed behind him.

The box was longer than it was wide and Jimmy couldn't help compared it in his mind to a coffin. Maybe, he thought, if he froze to death they could bury him in it. He wondered absently what might have been shipped in the crate. The walls were solid plywood and kept the wind and snow off of him. He huddled inside for a while, wondering about the phantom that had spotted him outside the shelter.

If he stayed in the box he might be safe. Cracking the make-shift door and peeking outside, Jimmy saw nothing. He crawled back inside, huddling for warmth away from the harsh wind. If he could survive the night, he might be able to go to the shelter and sleep the day and get something to eat.

Jimmy's stomach rumbled. He immediately wished he hadn't thought of food. He rubbed his mouth with his gloved hand. It had been a while since he'd eaten.

Jimmy peeked outside. It was dark. The butterscotch streetlights casted shapeless shadows across the brick and pavement. He didn't see any phantoms. As if to encourage him, his stomach rumbled. "Alright," he said, sliding out of the crate. He shut the door and kicked some snow to conceal the entrance. He would be gone an hour at the most.

The shelter was packed when Jimmy got there. He could see the phantoms floating over the heads of the other street people. They had chosen their victims. Jimmy tried not to look.

"Glad to see you came by," a voice said and Jimmy knew it was the flyer girl before he even turned to her.

"I...," Jimmy said and saw the phantom, his phantom, floating above her head.

"No," he said, backing away. He ran back out into the storm.

*****

In the crate, he lay on his back, covering his face with his hands. He had doomed that girl. Doomed her. He didn't even know her name. "Oh, God, I'm sorry."

The wind howled outside, rocking his crate. The wind howled again and he realized that it was not actually the wind. Jimmy inched the door open and looked outside.

A man dressed in frozen rags leaned against the brick wall of the alley. The phantom hung above him, its impossibly long fingers reached into the man's flesh, yanking bloody strands of light from him.

His soul?

Jimmy shut the door. His hand was shaking. He balled his hands into fists. The wind caught the door and yanked it open. He caught sight of the man, the last that anyone would ever see of him, as the phantom yanked him off the ground and went flying off into the night. The man's screams froze and fell like bloody snow.

Jimmy yanked the door shut again.

"The girl," he said, wiping his sweaty face with a near-frozen hand. What the hell was he going to do? "Something," he said, kicking the door back open.

When he got back to the shelter, the girl was gone.

"Excuse me," he said to one of the others. "Did you see the girl?"

"Uh, which girl?"

"Green hair?"

"Bailey?"

Bailey.

"I saw her go outside for a smoke," the guy said.

Jimmy ran.

He pushed out the back door and found Bailey leaning against the brick wall beneath a cloud of cigarette smoke. With her free hand she was catching butterfly-sized snowflakes. "Uh, hi," she said. "You okay?"

"You're in danger," he said.

She glared at her cigarette. "Coffin nails, I know," she said. "I'm trying to quit, but..."

"No," Jimmy said and tried to think how to explain the phantoms without sounding crazy. He didn't think there was a way. "I mean..."

The phantom appeared out of the shadows above Bailey's head. It reared back to strike.

Jimmy shoved Bailey out of the way.

"What the fuck, dude?" She fell backwards onto the ground, her feet slipping out from under her on the slick pavement.

Jimmy braced himself for the phantom's assault, but it did not come. The phantom hung in the air before him. He could not see the thing's face, but he could tell, somehow, that it was smiling at him.

He had to force himself to look away. On the frozen ground, Bailey wasn't moving. He got to his knees and gently lifted her head. Beneath his fingers he could feel the shattered bits of her skull. She was already growing cold. The blood was almost frozen. "Bailey," he said, softly, knowing that she would not answer.

The phantom dipped its long fingers into her chest like a Catholic blessing himself in holy water. It pulled her soul free without any pain or effort. It slipped the light into its face, devouring her.

Jimmy fell back away from her, holding up his bloody hands. The snowflakes landed in the blood, turning pink and then red-black as they soaked in the girl's blood.

Nightmares Every Night

"Hannah isn't dead," Blake said, sitting in his expensive car in front of his expensive house in his expensive subdivision that, at the moment, didn't really mean shit. "She isn't dead." He had to say it, had to actually hear it. "Fifteen years old," he said. She was under sedation in the psychiatric ward of the hospital that she had been born in. It only took twenty minutes to drive home, but Blake flipped his cellphone open and speed dialed Lillian.

"She's okay. I think." His wife hung up.

Blake sniffed and smoothed his hair back with both hands. The house, empty and dark, looked so distant and lonely, that he didn't even want to go inside. Why the hell had he even come home? "The blood." His shirt was soaked. They'd given him a scrub top in the emergency room, but his arms and neck were still maroon with dried blood. "My little girl."

The door swung open when Blake went to unlock it. The EMT's and the police had not locked it when they left. It didn't matter. Blake dropped the keys on a table in the foyer and collapsed onto an antique bench in the hall.

He stared at the basement door. Hannah's bedroom door. Blake had the basement finished as a surprise for her birthday. He grinned, thinking about her hysterical reaction. He could feel her arms around his neck, hear her laughter. Blake's grin faded and he gritted his teeth. He sprung up from the bench, threw open the door and stomped down the stairs. Fat spots of blood dotted the lavender carpet. He stepped around them.

Hannah kept her room in immaculate condition and except for the blood on the floor and the few items that the emergency workers disturbed, it was still perfect. Her posters of artwork lined the walls neatly. Her books were stacked in a bookshelf made of cinder blocks and boards and she'd made her bed before slitting her wrists.

Blake had only meant to take the blanket off the bed. It was soaked with blood and he had meant to change it so when Hannah came back it would not upset her. He tugged at it, then pulled the whole mattress off, tossed it on the floor. Blake knocked the lamp off the night table, pulled open the drawer and dumped the contents on the floor. He knocked all the books to the floor and, grunting with the effort, tossed one of the cinder blocks against the opposite wall, punching a hole in the drywall.

He sat on the bare box spring, breathing heavily. He looked over at the pile of personal belongings from the nightstand and flushed with embarrassment. He scrambled to pick the things up. Lipstick, earrings without matches and a lone tampon. Three notebooks sat on the floor when everything was picked up. Blake stared at them, heart pounding. He picked one up, flipped open the battered cover. *Dream Journal.*

1/24 Nightmare: ...trapped in a lopsided house there's a man that is trying to kill me...

1/25 Nightmare:...the walls are closing in on me...I can't breathe...

1/26 Nightmare:...the man again...so many teeth...I think he wants to eat me...

Blake flipped through the pages. *Nightmare. Nightmare. Nightmare.* "Every single night," Blake said, his voice startling him. He grabbed the other notebooks and they all said the same thing. "She was having nightmares every single night since her last birthday." Blake had read that the stress of adolescence sometimes brought on schizophrenia. He neatly set the notebooks in his daughter's nightstand, fixed the lamp and went about picking up after his tantrum.

The cinder block stuck out from the wall like a loose tooth and he had to give it a real tug to free it. He examined the broken drywall. Maybe he could get somebody in, Edison, the guy who did the original work.

As he examined the wall, Blake noticed that something was written under the sheetrock. Carpenter's measurements maybe? He looked closer.

There was a crooked man...

Blake's hands were shaking. He pulled at the drywall, folding it back away from the two-by-four.

...who built a crooked house.

"What the fuck?" Blake kicked the drywall, splitting it. He pulled a chunk free. The wall underneath was covered in black marker.

There was a crooked man...crooked house...crooked man...who built a crooked house...

Distantly, he noticed that the walls were, in fact, not straight. They stuck out just a bit at the ceiling. They were actually very uneven. The more he watched them, the more uneven they seemed. "Crooked," he said. "They aren't uneven, they're crooked." Hands crusted with gypsum, Blake yanked another piece of drywall from the studs. The words were as disgusting as an insect infestation. One line was written twice as big as the others. Blake read it.

There was a little girl, who died in a crooked room.

"Who the fuck did the work on my house?"

On the phone, Edison, the general contractor, was awake, but not nearly enough. "Who...is this?"

"Hanley. Blake Hanley."

"Oh," Edison said, like he had just, at that moment, been diagnosed with an inoperable brain tumor. Was he expecting this call?

"Who did the work?"

"My crew..."

"Don't lie to me, Edison. I'm an attorney and I will sue you within an inch of your life. The next house you build will be made of cardboard boxes."

"We were overbooked, swamped, you have to understand..."

"I don't give a shit. Who did the actual work?" Blake found a pen on his desk.

"His name was Drum."

"What was his first name?"

"Um, Aiken. I think. Yeah. Aiken Drum."

Blake sat up in his chair. "Don't bullshit me, Edison. My daughter slit her wrists."

"Oh, God, I'm sorry. Listen, I swear on my mother, his name was Aiken Drum. I wrote the fucking checks..."

"Aiken Drum is a fairytale character. That's like saying Peter Pan did the plumbing."

"I've never heard of any fairytale. I don't have kids. Maybe if I had kids I would have understood."

"Yeah," Blake said. "Maybe you would. Give me his address."

"Give me a minute," Edison said.

While he waited for Edison, Blake went into his closet, opened the safe and removed his pistol. He kept it loaded. He double checked the weapon and went back to his desk. Edison returned after a moment with the address. "He didn't...touch her, did he?"

"Not the way you're thinking."

"Look, I know you're a lawyer and everything, but if the police ask?"

"I have a crooked wall that needs straightening." He hung up on Edison and dialed Lillian.

"The doctors can't wake her up, Blake, she won't wake up. She went into some kind of coma twenty minutes ago."

When he read the writing on the wall. "Watch her close," Blake said and ended the call.

In the darkness and silence of his office, Blake sat in his chair holding his gun and staring at the address. "Just so we're clear, your honor, I believe that this man, this Aiken Drum, somehow built nightmares into my little girl's room that led her to try to end her own life and further, your honor, I believe that confronting this man may, in some way, save my little girl's sanity and possibly her life."

The room was silent except for the sound of Blake's heartbeat. He put the address and the pen in his pocket, got up and went down to the car.

When he found Drum's house, he was not the least bit surprised. It was a two-family row house in a neighborhood that was in the process of being demolished. Drum's house leaned over as if it were eavesdropping on the ghosts of the unoccupied house next to it. A crooked house for a crooked man. Blake did not slow down as he passed it. "There was a man lived in the moon, in the moon, in the moon, there was a man lived in the moon and his name was Aiken Drum," he said.

He parked a block away and walked back, staying to the shadows as he went. It occurred to him that he might have established an alibi for himself, before he embarked on this little mission. He was being the kind of client he hated, guilty, with no forethought.

The house was dark, but the moon was round and bright and cast a strange luminescence that felt like winter even though it was the warm part of June. He expected to see the familiar face, but it looked wrong, as if he were seeing the alien moon of some far off planet.

Blake cut across an empty lot, nearly falling into an exposed basement in the dark. He hopped a rusty chain-link fence at the back, stopping at the top for a moment to get a look at the back of Drum's crooked house.

The house was dark except for the spots of light where the windows reflected the moonlight. If someone were standing in one of the windows watching him, he would have no way of knowing. He shivered despite the warm night. The house was two stories tall with an exposed basement in the back. A broken piece of plywood covered the basement door, in shadow beneath the back deck that looked like it might collapse at any moment.

Blake gently lowered himself to the ground. His eyes had adjusted to the dark and as he crossed the backyard, he thanked God that they had. The yard was strewn with scrap wood and salvaged junk. He stepped carefully, until he was in the shade of the porch.

A sound.

Blake froze, listening.

Keys? No.

He held his breath and stole a glance up between the rotten boards of the deck. Something twinkled in the moonlight. Wind chimes?

Several skeleton keys hung from wire above the back door. In the center, a cracked stain glass half-moon. Blake relaxed, forcing a smile.

The wind chimes twinkled again. An odd sound for an odd house. The sound seemed to get louder and louder. No breeze, Blake thought, watching the glass moon spin against the keys and nails that hung with it. "Was a man lived in the moon," he said, pulling the piece of plywood free. The door behind it was intact, though cracks spider-webbed the glass. Blake caught his distorted reflection in the glass and he thought that he looked like a crazy person. Not guilty due to mental disease or defect, your honor.

Blake removed his cellphone, flipped it open and went inside. The light from the screen lit up the basement. A virtual tunnel led through junk stacked on all sides. A mantle piece leaned against the wall, stacked with grimy brass light fixtures that looked like they could be a hundred years old. Heavy old doors leaned against the wall. Blake found the stairs and went up.

The basement door opened on the small kitchen. Blake could hear the wind chimes again as he slipped across the cracked tile floor. He doubted that any wind was blowing. An ancient cast iron stove dominated the kitchen. It looked like it could have belonged to the child-eating witch from Hansel and Gretel. For all Blake knew, she might live here, too.

so many teeth...I think he wants to eat me...

Blake drifted down the hallway past the bathroom and into the living room.

The room was piled with tools. Not the shiny stainless steel Craftsman tools that lined the walls of his garage. These tools were wood and iron, rusty with time and age and use. He recognized some, but not others. There were still more that didn't look like tools at all, at least not carpentry tools. Some looked like Victorian surgical implements or Civil War era dentist's tools. They looked used as well. Used for what, though?

Blake slid the gun out of his pocket and flipped off the safety.

The moonlight coming through the windows on the first floor was enough to see by and Blake returned the phone to his pocket. Upstairs, then.

The phone rang.

Blake scrambled to answer it. Hannah crying in the background. "Baby?"

No. Lillian's voice. "She cries in her sleep. Did you know that? She cries and she won't stop and she won't wake up."

Blake flipped the phone shut and turned the sound off. His hand shook as he returned the phone to his pocket. His fury had cooled and now seemed to grow into an icy cold fear in his belly. Blake looked at the gun. What the hell am I doing?

Hannah's crying again.

Blake reached for his phone, but realized that it wasn't coming from there.

He took the stairs two at a time. One hallway reached from the back of the house to the front. One end was the master bedroom and the other would have been the second bedroom. The crying was coming from there. He moved down the hall, cautiously passing another bathroom.

Blake pressed his head against the door.

"Daddy?"

"Hannah?"

"Oh, God, Daddy help me!"

Tears burned Blake's eyes. This wasn't possible. He flipped the phone open. "Lillian? Where's Hannah?"

"Blake, she stopped crying, honey, she stopped."

"*Where* is she?"

"What do you mean? She's...right...here." Blake flipped the telephone shut.

"Daddy?"

Blake crouched down on the floor. "Who are you?"

"Daddy, please, before he comes back."

"Who the fuck are you?"

"Daddy," she said and started crying again.

Blake dug his cellphone out, slid it under the door and snapped a picture. He pulled it back out and stared at it.

In the blurry picture, Hannah crouched on the floor on the other side of the door.

Blake grabbed the door handle and tried to pull it open. Locked. No, not just locked. Nailed shut. He pulled on it again. "I need to get a tool from downstairs."

"Please don't leave, please Daddy don't leave."

Her fingers poked out from under the door. Blake put the gun down. Hands shaking, he reached down and touched them. She grabbed him with all of her strength. "I'll be right back, honey, right back." Blake pulled himself free and hurried down the stairs.

The tools were as poorly organized as anything in the house. Blake threw open a wooden box full of chisels. He grabbed one, dropped it, picked up a bigger, sharper one. He needed a hammer. He found one, but something caught his eye.

An ax leaned against the wall, and Blake grabbed for it, but a hand snatched it away. "There was a crooked man..." With a voice as crooked as his body, he spoke as if he had no clue what the words meant and just happened to string them together. The arm that held the ax was longer than the other and the left leg seemed longer than the right, forcing him over and balancing the weight of the ax. One eye dwarfed the other and it stared at Blake in the dark.

"Aiken Drum." Blake remembered that he'd left the gun upstairs.

Drum smiled a lopsided smile, like he had once had a stroke, and considered the ax in his hands. "You are not a man that *works with his hands*, are you?"

145

"I'm taking my daughter and leaving."

"Are you? Well, don't let me stop you." He flung open the front door.

Blake could see the street.

"Maybe, not, then" Drum said, gently closing the door and locking several deadbolts and a chain. He looked at the ax again. "I would like it, if it is all the same to you, if you would scream when this happens. There isn't another soul for miles and no one would hear you. There is nothing to be ashamed of, I mean."

Blake ran.

Something caught his foot and sent him sprawling face down on the floor. He could taste blood in his mouth. The pen in his breast pocket jabbed into his chest.

Drum took slow, uneven steps across the floor behind him. "There was a crooked man..."

"Hannah," Blake said.

"Daddy."

Blake pulled the pen out of his shirt, clutching it, hoping that he might get a moment to stab Drum in the neck with it, knowing that he would not.

"...who had a crooked ax..." Drum raised the ax above his head.

Blake stared at the wall, unable to move. The wall. Blake reached out with the pen and scratched out words on the yellow wallpaper. "There was a crooked man that died in a crooked house," he said breathlessly.

He heard drum's massive weight hit the floor behind him.

Blake got to his feet.

Drum wasn't dead. He writhed on the floor, trying to get back up.

Blake got the gun, but knew that it would do no good. Instead, he took his pen and went back to the wall, repeating the phrase that had felled the monster in the first place. Repeating it until the man named Aiken Drum stopped breathing.

Blake stood over the body for a long time before he took the ax upstairs and hacked the door down. The room was empty as he expected it to be. The phone vibrated in his pocket. "Yeah," he said, listening to the music of his daughter's voice on the other end.

<u>ABOUT THE AUTHOR</u>

Gary Buettner lives in Indiana with his wife and kids. He is also the author of a middle-grade spooky adventure series, Monster Pets.

Made in the USA
Columbia, SC
18 May 2021